DESERT SKIES, REBEL SOULS

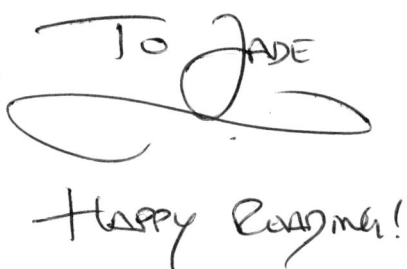

To Jade

Happy Reading!

M.P. Tonnesen

ISBN: 1977695302
ISBN 13: 9781977695307

To all the rebels and adventurers
To all the dreamers and lovers
To my grandmother who taught me to be a lady and to open
my heart to others

1

S he did not regret anything. Except leaving him. It had not been her intention. They had become victims of the circumstances. She had gone back for him. And that had made all the difference.

Worse than unrequited love was loving someone lost. Even worse was not knowing if that someone was lost forever.

They provided modest accommodation, their small barracks on the outskirts of the kibbutz. Four identical blocks were lined up one after another like magnolia dominoes with views of the fields and the guesthouses where old people stayed in the hope of obtaining eternal life from the hot springs nearby.

Depending on the wind direction, any given day you could smell the excrement of the turkeys, the urine of the bulls or the sulphur of the hot springs. Olivia still had not decided which of the three sources of income gave off the least appalling stench.

The sun was beginning to peek over the big carob trees shading the communal building. From the little concrete step outside the door she picked up her black work shoes, adjacent to those of her two roommates. They were still sleeping in their narrow beds, squeezed into the one spartan room they shared. She was on the early morning shift in the kitchen: preparing toast, tea and coffee, cutlery and crockery, and all the other essentials before the rest of the kitchen team arrived to complete the breakfast for the kibbutzniks and guests.

She shook her shoes, checking for scorpions and other creepy-crawlies. She had preferred to keep her shoes indoors, but their smell was overwhelming; a constant reminder of the numerous volunteers who had worn them before her.

A bird greeted her good morning from above; a slight, cool breeze caressed her cheek. She looked up towards the horizon where the dusty, brown hills were still covered in fluffy cotton plants waiting for the imminent harvest. Olivia wondered what lay on the other side.

She had needed to escape. She had needed a break from performing and pandering to the expectations of others.

Olivia had stood on her own at the top of the escalators waving goodbye to her family and Daniel, her high school sweetheart; then taken the first step of her longest walk through Copenhagen Airport to the gate of the EL-AL flight waiting to sweep her away on her Middle-Eastern journey. Her grandmother had cried and acted as if she would never see her again. Daniel had clung to her like a great poison ivy, winding up her trunk for support. Her mother had given her a couple of extra pecks on the cheek. Olivia had noticed the tightness of her mother's smile, surprised she was even there.

Her father had hugged her longer than usual, then said matter-of-factly, "If there's any trouble, you contact the Danish consulate."

And that was it. She was off on her first adventure abroad. Alone.

The warm, dry air wrapped around her, embalming her first steps onto Israeli ground. Never before had she experienced being surrounded by people speaking a language which she did not know – except from the few basic phrases of courtesy she had learned by heart from her pocket dictionary on the plane. The first one came in handy at the border control.

"*Toda.*" She beamed as she was handed back her passport. The dark-haired, stout policeman did not seem impressed, though, as he waved her through impatiently.

Olivia hefted her bursting backpack from the conveyor belt. She was greeted by a lady from the agency through which she had applied to become a kibbutz volunteer. A small handful of young people were gathered around her: a couple and two girls who Olivia had heard speaking Danish together on the plane. They turned out to be travelling on their own as well.

"Welcome to Israel." The lady smiled and guided them to a minivan waiting for them outside the arrivals hall. "I will take you to the office where we will go through your options. Then you will spend the night at a hostel nearby before you go to your chosen kibbutz tomorrow morning. Okay?" Olivia nodded absentmindedly while she processed the heavy accent of this petite, middle-aged lady. She turned her head to absorb the exotic impressions radiating towards her from outside the tinted windows as the vehicle sped through the landscape. Palm trees swaying; houses in shades of white, beige and sand; orthodox believers in black; military believers in green. She was surprised at how modern everything looked. To be honest, she had not really known what to expect. She was ashamed to admit that the limited knowledge she had of the place was from the volunteers' agency brochures, supplemented by her history and religious education classes at school. It was bound to be dated, not to mention stereotypical.

"So, have you decided what kind of kibbutz you want to go to?" The agent was greeted with silence as the random group of young Danes looked hesitantly at each other in the small office. It was no insignificant decision. They had probably all spent most of their savings on flight tickets and agency fees. Their great expectations for the months to come were hard to contain within these four bland walls, sparsely decorated with a couple of posters displaying smiling young people picking oranges in the sun. Judging by the similar ages of the anxious group members, this was their coming-of-age journey. There was no room for blunders. Whatever choice they made within the next moments would shape their entire adventure. Olivia had heard from others back home that the big kibbutzim in the north were pretty much synonymous with volunteer parties twenty-four-seven. She was more inclined to go to a smaller kibbutz where she would get a chance to really mingle with the locals and get the full cultural experience she was hoping for.

"Any preferences where in the country you would like to live?" The lady tried again as she placed a pile of binders on her desk.

"Maybe a smaller kibbutz if possible, please?" Olivia ventured.

"Okay. I have some available spaces in a large kibbutz near Haifa, and three spaces available in a small one near Ashqelon which is south of Tel Aviv, but not too far."

"I…"

"We…"

They all spoke at once, having finally mustered the courage.

The couple – or friends or whatever the relationship between the tall, lanky, ginger guy and the short, dark-haired girl was – looked at one another and said: "We would really like to go to the big kibbutz. Together."

"That's fine. Here is the information I've got on it." The agent handed them a few sheets of paper. "And you three? Are you travelling together?"

Olivia and the two girls glanced at each other, fidgeting and shifting in their seats.

"Well, no. But I think I would like to go to the small kibbutz too," the sturdy built, light blonde girl said, smiling at Olivia.

"Me too," the waify, medium blonde joined in.

"Well, that's all settled then." The agent clasped her hands with a satisfied smile. Her job was done. "If you could all just fill out these forms, I will fax your information to the two kibbutzim. Then I think it's dinner time."

Hannah and Lola were their names; they sounded like the names of the two puppets – Anna and Lotte – in the popular Danish children's programme their generation had grown up watching in the seventies and eighties. The whole group had laughed for a while at this over dinner. *Two's company, three's a crowd*, Olivia could hear her mother's voice in her head, but she was keeping her hopes up for this new constellation now destined for the same little spot on the map.

Their meal consisted of pita breads with kebab, hummus or falafel – the latter the national dish apparently. The five of them dined under fluorescent lights, seated on plastic chairs outside a falafel shop around the corner from the hostel. Surrounded by the sounds of traffic and foreign languages, the young Danes marvelled at the contrast of the bustling local scenery to their peaceful home country.

Olivia was dreading spending the night in a bunk bed in a room full of strangers. She had not been too comfortable with leaving her backpack there when they had gone out. Her passport and money were resting safely in her neck purse, though. The shekels felt heavy around her neck. She had exchanged a note for coins and phoned her parents from the hostel's payphone. Their brief conversation had added an unexpected pang of longing to her passing disquiet. She had brushed it all off and ventured into the streets with her unfamiliar companions.

She got her camera out to immortalise the moment. It was a leaving present from Daniel: a compact Canon with just enough functionality for her to be able to play around with light and perspective when documenting her adventures. She made sure the date function was on, got the group's attention and said the mandatory "Smile!" Her first entry in her photo diary: two people she would never see again; plus two individuals with whom she had thrown in her lot by chance to explore the world.

As the dust settled from the departing minivan, the three girls looked up at the wooden sign arching over the entrance to their new home. They were unable to decipher the strange letters, but picked up their backpacks and their courage then stepped under the arch like pioneers venturing into the unknown.

There were forms to fill, fees to pay, stamps to obtain, followed by clothes and shoes to pick from the mounds of used volunteer work outfits. Olivia momentarily felt like she was in a refugee camp, the feeling exacerbated when she was informed of her number.

"One-five-six," the voluminous, older woman spelled out while pointing to a green label in the neck of a washed-out T-shirt. Olivia looked at her inquiringly, trying her best to be polite and inoffensive.

"Sorry? I don't understand."

"Your number for laundry!" the woman exclaimed with exasperation in a surprising accent. Was that Spanish or Portuguese? Olivia was still unsure as to what exactly this number referred. The younger woman, who had escorted the girls through the kibbutz from the administrative office, smiled and explained in her Hebrew-American accent:

"You hand in your dirty clothes at the communal laundry every Tuesday morning, and then you can usually pick it up by the end of the following day."

"Oh, I see. But what about our own clothes? They don't have any numbers in them."

"Don't worry." She winked. "Volunteers hand in all their laundry as a group, so you should be able to sort out which is which when you get it back." The young woman's name was Yael, and she looked strikingly similar to most of the young Israeli females Olivia had seen during her limited time in her new country: short to medium height; long, dark, wavy hair; almond-shaped, brown eyes; slender waist and voluptuous bust. The army girls in particular looked like fierce and foxy Amazons with M16s casually draped down their backs. So surreal – and a far cry from the average Scandinavian female. Not that Olivia was the standard blonde Viking woman herself.

Yael had shown them to their barracks and left them with her direct number.

"If you have any questions and there's no one in the office, you can call me from the phone hanging outside its door."

The three Danish girls had been assigned to work in the kitchen and *cheder ochel* – the communal building where everyone had their meals. Only tomorrow would tell whatever that entailed. For now they were retiring to their shoebox of a room, casually unpacking their few personal belongings, digesting their first hours of impressions.

"I don't get it," Olivia sighed, lying on her back in her narrow metal bed. "How can they be so skinny, yet have such big boobs? It's physically impossible!"

"It must be something they eat." Lola giggled.

"Like what?" Hannah sounded sceptical as she inspected the inside of their joint wardrobe.

"Like… avocados?" Olivia speculated.

"Or maybe mangos?" Lola pitched in.

"Whatever it is, they sure must be eating a lot of it!" Olivia concluded. They all laughed as they now each lay pondering what kind of food they clearly should be eating more of – starting tomorrow. Right now they were keen to explore their new surroundings. The travel dust still clung to their skin. They ventured outside in search of the swimming pool.

Olivia knew she cut quite a noticeable figure at the pool herself, with her push-up bikini enhancing her modest chest, and her miniscule sundress revealing long, slender legs. She was aware of the looks she got from the local guys and volunteers alike. A life guard with mirrored shades watched the small crowd splayed out on the patches of green grass. He was an older guy, mid to late twenties with long, curly hair tied in a ponytail.

The Danish trio had joined a group of five other volunteers – all British – who had arrived a few days before. The atmosphere around the pool was full of excitement, the three guys cracking jokes whilst drinking from beer cans in the late afternoon sun. Olivia leaned back in the spiky grass taking in the scene with a satisfied sigh.

Mangos. She noticed the skilful way in which he was able to peel and dissect them with ease. A local guy seated at one of the white plastic tables. He looked like a solitary rock with his well-built frame and dark, crew-cut hair shining in the sun, lounging by himself withdrawn from the crowd.

"Want some?" His voice was a distinct melange of gentle and rough, the outcome husky and sexy.

"Excuse me?"

"Want some mango?" He gestured at the ripe, yellow flesh on the frayed piece of tissue in front of him. "You've been staring at it for a while, so thought I'd better offer you a piece." He had a mischievous smile on his lips. She suddenly felt self-conscious, caught in the act of observing him. Still, her curiosity was too piqued to decline his offer.

"Yes, actually. Would love some, thank you." She put a stray lock of hair behind her ear as she got up from the grass. "We don't get a lot of mangos where I'm from."

"Where is that then?" His accent was alluring. The throaty Hebrew hint to the American English which seemed to be the standard for young people here.

She bit into the wet piece of fruit. The juice ran down her chin and hands, making it impossible for her to carry on the conversation in a civilised manner. Her eyes caught his and they both chuckled.

"Here."

She was distracted by the tanned flesh he exposed under his white T-shirt as he leaned over to hand her a tissue. *Nice abs.*

"Pretty messy this mango stuff."

"Life is messy." He shrugged, flexing one eyebrow. "I'm Chaim. Life in Hebrew."

"I guess you know what you're talking about then." She winked and immediately regretted it. She swallowed and steadied her jittery legs. "I'm Olivia." She tasted his name in her mouth briefly, then let out a small laugh as the unexpected connection dawned on her. "Liv actually means life in Danish! What are the odds?"

"Huh, is that so? Well, it's nice to meet you, Olivia from Denmark." He nodded with a smile as he leaned back. She could feel his eyes on her half-naked body, discreetly taking her in. She got an inexplicable fluttering sensation in her stomach.

"So, what do you do around here? When you're not peeling mangos."

He smirked. "I kill time." The matter-of-fact tone of his voice made him sound like an assassin. "I finished school in July, and now I'm helping with the cotton harvest until I have to start the army." He seemed older than any eighteen or nineteen-year-old guys she knew back home.

"Oh, the army, of course." Olivia thought of all the young soldiers she had seen on her journey from when she landed at the airport till she arrived at the kibbutz. "When?"

"November."

She did the maths in her head. Three months from now.

Her thoughts were interrupted by Hannah's voice. "Olivia, the shop's open. Do you want to come with us and check it out?"

Olivia turned her head to look at the others getting up and gathering their things. A drop of sweat trickled down her back to rest between her buttocks as she contemplated whether to join them.

"Good to meet you." Chaim slid his shades back on. Olivia tilted her head as she caught her own reflection in the dark glass.

"Likewise." She smiled and got up. "I'll see you around?"

"Sure." He nodded and returned her smile as he leaned back in the white plastic chair.

She caught up with the others, grabbed her sundress from the ground and pulled it over her head, smoothed her wavy, brown bob and sent him a look over her shoulder as she bounced off in the direction of the small convenience store.

The store was tiny and cool, dimly lit by a few fluorescent tubes from the low ceiling. A small cold counter was humming on the left, stocking dairy. A short row of shelves in the middle of the room displayed snacks, candy and toiletries. A few shelves on the back wall housed beer and wine. All labels adorned with the swirly letters of this strange language which Olivia was keen to learn. She grabbed a couple of bananas from a green plastic crate on the floor. She grinned when she spotted a mango and picked it up.

"Really into mangos, aren't you?" Charlie, a tall, blonde Brit nudged her with his shoulder and grinned.

"What can I say – they're nice and sweet." Olivia shrugged with a coy smile.

"Tricky to eat, though." He winked, placing his beer bottles and bags of potato crisps on the counter. "155, please."

The cashier nodded and flicked through a small box of yellow note cards, pulled out one with only a few scribbles and wrote down the total amount of Charlie's goods after adding them up on a calculator.

"Funny – I'm 156."

"Hey, Number Neighbour!" Charlie beamed and put his hand in the air, his open palm inviting hers to high-five it. She chuckled and played along. *Quite the joker, this one.*

"Aren't you getting any drinks for tonight?"

"Tonight?"

"Yeah, we're having a 'housewarming' party at James, Aidan and my place to celebrate the arrival of The New

Batch." Charlie marked housewarming with air quotes and emphasised his last words with a theatrical tone. "Maybe you missed this while you were off meeting the locals." He wiggled his eyebrows.

"Maybe I did." His insinuations got on Olivia's nerves. Was he trying to make her feel guilty? She had only just met him, and he did not even know that she had a boyfriend at home.

"So, are you up for a party?"

"Sure. Always." She was exhausted by now, but did not want to miss out on the group action. She walked to the back wall and grabbed a couple of beer bottles with a gold star on the label. That would do. She shivered in her thin dress as she placed her stuff on the counter.

"Hey, let me warm you with a Charlie-cuddle. Always does the trick."

Before she could object he had his arms wrapped around her, rocking her from side to side. Her eyes darted around the shop. She was relieved to discover the others had left already. He smelt surprisingly good considering they had been sitting in the sun for hours. She got conscious of her own sweaty body and withdrew. Charlie's eyes caught hers. They were sparkling green like sea glass in the sun.

"Better?"

She nodded.

"Now let's get out of here and get the party started!" He grabbed her hand and pulled her out of the shop, their plastic bags of bottles tinkling in the twilight stillness as they ran across the lawn.

The group had divided into those who got changed – mainly the girls – and those who continued straight into the more serious drinking outside the barracks.

Olivia was starving and desperately needed a shower.

"See you in a jiffy!" Charlie called after her in a playful tone as she went into her room. She sent him a smile over her shoulder.

"Did you buy the whole shop?" Hannah was filling up a drawer with the remaining contents of her backpack. She had showered and changed already.

"I didn't know about the party till Charlie told me, so had to rethink my shopping…"

"Cute, that Charlie guy." Lola twittered, stepping out of the tiny bathroom, her long hair enveloped in a towel turban.

Olivia put her fruit in the small fridge and did not reply, too busy eating a banana.

"The bottom drawer and the two top shelves in the closet are yours." Hannah shut her drawer and slid her empty backpack under her bed.

"Good thing we're all travelling light," Olivia remarked as she opened the closet to take stock of where to put her belongings. She did not have time to unpack fully now. She would have to focus on getting ready to join the others and leave it till the morning to get organised. "Are we not going to have dinner?" The banana did a brave, but futile job at filling her stomach.

"Don't think anyone's bothered. I had a few snacks from the shop." Lola was strutting around in her bright pink lace underwear, brushing her hair. "Don't want to miss out on the fun!" she giggled.

No wonder the Brits had a reputation for getting plastered if they always drank on an empty stomach. Olivia was torn. She knew all too well how the evening would develop if she did not get more than a piece of fruit in her before diving into full-on drinking. She also wanted to check out the dining hall prior to starting work tomorrow and be in a decent state for her first day. *Well, at least we don't have to start till 9am...*

She thought of Chaim as she stood in the shower. Was he in the dining hall now? Maybe looking for her? Would he be there tomorrow? Why did she even care? His eyes were light-brown, a stark contrast to his dark hair. They had been serious, but not unkind – hesitant to give anything away. She pictured his athletic frame in a uniform. He would be perfect for the job.

"Olivia, we're heading over to the guys now!" Hannah called from the other side of the door. "See you there."

"Yep, I'll be right with you!" She really had to get her act together.

The laughter was loud and the fun in full swing when Olivia joined the party. A small tape player in an open window contributed to the festive atmosphere.

"Hey, it's my favourite Dane!" Charlie greeted her with open arms. Olivia stopped in her tracks. Her eyes caught Lola's which twinkled back at her. *Oh, boy.*

She sat down next to Charlie, in the only spare seat, and went with the cheerful flow of beers and banter.

Charlie's arm soon found its way around her shoulder as the eight of them sat under the stars in plastic chairs or on the ground, sharing bits and pieces about themselves and their lives, sprinkled with jokes and amusing anecdotes.

Charlie was a trust fund baby rebelling against his family. His stories hit a bit too close to home for Olivia's taste. He was twenty-two and still had not figured out what he wanted out of life despite his bachelor's degree in business. James was a young, full-blown socialist who had decided to pursue his calling in more exotic surroundings than his hometown of Hull could provide. Aidan was a quiet guy. He came from a farm and preferred to drink his beer in peace, joining in with a few jokes and a chuckle now and then. Olivia struggled to place his accent until he revealed he was from Northern Ireland. Pippa and Bridget were the two English roses. Both had pale skin and round features, one dark haired and the other ginger. Bridget had glasses and wanted to study geography after her gap year. Pippa giggled so much that it was hard to understand much of what she eventually said. History was going to be her major, was all Olivia gathered. They were a lovely bunch, all of them. It was a mind-boggling notion that they had all ventured out on their own into the unknown and had converged to this tiny dot on the planet at the exact same time. Olivia leaned back to look up at the stars and felt Charlie's arm behind her neck.

"Beautiful," he whispered in her ear.

"Yes, they are indeed." The bright expanse of little sparkles in the sky was phenomenal.

"I meant you."

The alcohol from the beers and shots, with which her new friends had taken turns to top her up after she had emptied her own two golden bottles, rushed to her head.

"Charlie, I…"

"Don't worry. You don't have to say I'm beautiful too. I know."

Olivia erupted in laughter. *Always ready with a joke, this guy.*

"I think it's time for me to go to bed. It's been a looong day."

"Shall I walk you home?"

"My room is like ten steps away!"

"Still, you never know what lurks in the dark."

"All right then." Olivia had a strong feeling he would not take no for an answer. She tried to ignore the curious eyes of the others when they both got up and left the party. He kept his arm around her shoulder as they walked along the narrow path. He still smelt nice.

"Goodnight, Charlie." She removed his arm from her shoulder and turned to enter her room. He laced his fingers with hers and pulled her back. Her head was spinning and she nearly fell, but he caught her with his other arm and held her tight. She could feel the heat from his body and his breath. His eyes refused to let go of hers. She could hear the cheerful voices and the faint music only a few feet away, yet hidden behind some bushes. He kissed her and she surrendered. It was a gentle kiss. Comforting, uplifting and risk-free. His tongue testing the new territory, awaiting her reaction. He was a gentleman after all.

"Goodnight, Olivia," he whispered as she broke away, his forehead still against hers before she finally stepped up on the concrete stoop.

"See you tomorrow." She waved with a smile and closed the door behind her.

What a day!

2

The laundry lady and quite a few other members of the kibbutz turned out to originate from Argentina. From Olivia's perspective, this was not the most obvious place of origin for immigrants in Israel. However, she soon learned that in fact there was a large Jewish diaspora in Argentina, initially following the Jewish expulsion from Spain, but later originating from all over Europe. Following the deadly 1994 AMIA bombing in Buenos Aires attacking the Jewish community, and in the wake of the Argentine political and economic crisis in the late 1990s, many Argentine Jews emigrated to Israel in search of a better life. Olivia was fascinated by how her path had now merged with theirs.

The passionate cook, Mateo, was Argentinian too. His laugh was as loud as his yell. The Danish girls had joined Pippa and Bridget in the kitchen for their initial day of duty. Poor Lola had been the first victim of his temper. She had been given a recipe for a cake and happily mixed all the ingredients of the batter in one bowl. Little did she know that kosher rules were applied in the kitchen – mainly for the benefit of the paying visitors in the guest houses. This custom required cracking the eggs open in a separate bowl to check them all for red dots. Red dots on the yolk meant it had been contaminated with blood which instantly made it non-kosher. Olivia gathered that much from the multilingual tirade unfolding in front of her. Lola was on the verge of tears, but Mateo gave her a pat on the shoulder and said *"Zeh b'seder"* – it's okay – before he discarded the entire contents of the industrial mixing bowl.

Olivia was surprised that a secular environment like a socialist kibbutz honoured religion in this way. Perhaps the world was not as black and white as she had been raised to think.

"It's learning by doing." She gave Lola an encouraging smile.

"I guess so," Lola sniffled and opened a new box of eggs.

Olivia was assigned to the dining hall. She was to serve meals and keep the entire communal building clean – including the toilets on the ground floor. A pretty local girl called Naomi was showing her the ropes. She was eighteen too, but her English was limited. This provided Olivia with the perfect way to learn Hebrew, one word at the time. Salads were *Salatim*, water was *Mayim*, and soap was *Sabon*. Three new words per day became her objective. She was excited to be given the chance to interact with so many different people every day and tried desperately to not let her cleaning duties get her down. The toilets were the ultimate low point. She was surprised at how hard it was for some people to actually hit the bowl, let alone use a toilet brush. *You can't win them all*, she sighed as she pulled on her rubber gloves.

"Old people. And kids." Naomi pointed at the brown smudges on a toilet seat.

The girls scrunched their faces at each other in agreement. At least they took turns. One did the floors while the other did the toilets; the next day they swapped. Six days a week. They developed a great partnership with few words spoken, the silence supplemented by voices from the kitchen, and the small radio playing the latest local and international hits.

It was Friday before she saw him again.

"*Ma yesh bee'mkmom? Lemata?*" An old lady stared at Olivia, clearly expecting an answer. Olivia was sweating from arranging the hot food trays on the heating trolley.

"I'm sorry, I don't understand. *Lo mevina*," she quickly recalled her go-to expression when in doubt.

"She's asking what's instead. Below in the heating drawer."

Olivia jumped at the sound of his voice. She smiled sheepishly. Why did she have to be sweating every time she met him?

"I guess she's not happy with the food on the menu." Chaim gleamed in return. *That smile!*

"Cheeky, these old people." Olivia wiped her forehead with the back of her hand and tried to indicate to the lady that the food was all the same. She scoffed and moved along, her white-haired head shaking.

"How about you? Are you happy with what's on display?" Olivia straightened and tossed her brown tresses out of her eyes.

Chaim fixed her with his gaze. It was impossible for her to look away.

"Yes," he replied. "I like what I see." Olivia was not usually the blushing type, yet she could feel the heat prickling not only on her face, but all over her body. *Damned heating trolley!*

She cast down her eyes and served him a portion of the chicken stew and rice.

"Any plans for tonight?" It was her first weekend here and she was keen to find out what the locals got up to. This one in particular.

Chaim shrugged. "There's a disco on at the neighbouring kibbutz. Maybe I'll go with some friends."

A group of little naughty fairies struck up a jig in her stomach.

"Disco? Sounds like fun! Should we join them, Liv?" Charlie's voice cut through her excitement. She had avoided him all week. "Or are you a busy bee tonight too?"

Olivia cleared her throat. Her eyes flickered from Charlie to Chaim. Chaim gave her a nod and a subdued smile, then went off to eat his lunch with a group of local guys.

"Huh! Guess we won't be hitching a ride to the party with that guy!" Charlie smacked his lips.

"What do you want, Charlie?"

"Been off in the fields with my miserable packed lunches all week, so thought I'd take the chance and say hello to you today."

"Hello." Olivia smiled politely. "Now, what would you like to eat? You are holding up the queue."

"Right. Don't want to keep your other diners waiting. I'll have what that guy is having." He nodded in the direction of Chaim who was staring at her, his soulful eyes twinkling, despite the active conversation taking place among his surrounding friends.

She had not phoned her family or Daniel since she arrived in Tel Aviv. It seemed like every second had been filled to the brink since then and her life back home so distant already. Her chest tightened at the thought of them all. She had a moment now after dinner before she met up with the other volunteers for drinks.

He was a fantastic guy, Daniel. Her parents certainly approved. But he was predictable in every way: his conservative clothes, his ambitious career plans, his harmless jokes – even the sex followed a well tried and tested template. He had been her first. Was he going to be her last? He would have joined her on whatever adventure she had planned had he not been forced to enlist in the Danish army, which was mandatory for all eighteen-year-old males at the time – unless you drew a free ticket in the number allocation lottery. She was glad to be on her own, though. For so many reasons.

She picked up the receiver of the payphone just outside the dining hall. *A bit of privacy would have been nice...*

"Hi, it's me."

"Olivia!"

She nearly cried at the sound of relief in her father's voice.

"Sorry, I haven't called sooner, but it has been such a busy week, settling in and all."

"Well, as long as you're safe and sound." Her father was back to his composed self. "Your mother is still at work. Think she had a board meeting today."

"Oh…" Olivia swallowed.

"So, how is the kibbutz?"

"It's nice. People are nice. I mainly work in the dining room as a kind of waitress…"

"A waitress? At a farm?" The sense of incredulity and scepticism booming into her ear was almost tangible.

"Well, maybe not exactly a waitress, but I serve food and take out the dishes…" She could not bring herself to tell him about the dirty floors and toilets she was scrubbing too. "It's all good. I get to meet a lot of different people, and I'm picking up a bit of Hebrew already too, so…"

"Hmm…" She could hear her father processing how to add this to her future CV in the most advantageous way. "Good, good."

"I'm running out of coins, Dad. Maybe you or *Maman* could call me in a week's time? I will write you a letter with my address and the phone number."

"Oh! Yes, do that. Well, take care."

"Will do. Bye, Dad." She felt a tug at her heart. She looked at her watch. She would have to call Daniel tomorrow.

Their volunteer spirits were high as they sat on the back of the pickup truck. Yael was kindly giving them a lift to the neighbouring kibbutz. The sulphur smell of the hot springs lingered in the warm air of the night, giving rise to plenty of immature banter from the guys.

Olivia coughed after taking a swig of the bottle of cheap vodka being passed around.

"Good stuff, eh?" Charlie wiggled his eyebrows. His hand covered hers when she passed the bottle on to him. "Bet you've never tried anything like this at home!"

She could feel the raw alcohol burning down her throat, and her back hurt as they hit another pothole in the road. "That would be safe to say."

"So, any free spaces on your dance card tonight, princess?"

"Maybe." Olivia shrugged with a coy smile. Even in the darkness Charlie's green eyes sparkled. She could feel his muscular thigh against hers. *Rugby player maybe? That's what British boys do, right?*

Their ride came to an abrupt stop and she was thrown against his chest.

"Sorry," she giggled.

"That's perfectly all right. You can hang out on me any-time." His arms encompassed her in a swift move. The others were jumping off the truck, eager to dive into the kaleido-scope of lights, music and people welcoming them from in-side the large, industrial-looking hall. Charlie helped her to her feet and held on to her hand while she climbed over the sides as adroitly as she could in her tipsy state.

The bass notes of Bon Jovi's *Livin' On A Prayer* were thumping as Olivia spun around on the dance floor, her arms stretched out to the side, her eyes closed, her lips parted, humming along in uninhibited ecstasy. She opened her eyes briefly when the song ended and spotted him across the dance floor. Chaim was watching her with a smile. Her heart skipped a beat. Their eyes locked for what felt like an eternity. Those alluring brown eyes. She broke into a big grin and returned to her dancing with the other volunteer girls, loudly singing along as Counting Crows came on and *Mr Jones* blasted through the speakers. A hand grabbed hers. Endorphins rushed through her veins as she turned to face its owner.

"So, about that dance…" Charlie twirled her confidently into his arms. She tittered and wriggled free, continuing her uncommitted freestyle moves. He played along, bouncing and bopping till the music faded over to a crooning love song. Charlie pulled her closer and swayed her to the enamouring tones. She could feel his warm breath on her face. She turned her head, her eyes searching the room. Charlie grabbed her shoulders gently.

"Look, Liv. I know you're pretending to be someone else, but I see you. We're the same, you and me. You can try all you want, but you can never run away from your family, your breed. Trust me, I have tried – and am still trying. But people like us, we belong somewhere else."

Olivia's smile faded. "I don't know what you're talking about. I need some air." She brushed off his hands and left the dance floor.

She ran her fingers along the wall as she walked down the corridor from the toilets towards the bar, as if the sensation of the rough plastering alone would be able to distract her from the overwhelming desire burning through her body after seeing Chaim here. Charlie and his whole "I know you" speech was an annoying distraction. They had only been in the kibbutz together for a week. He was a nice guy, but he did not know her at all. She hardly knew herself, and she was sick of being labelled. The good girl. The clever girl. The rich girl. She had to break free. Her mind was galloping again with indecent thoughts. She needed a glass of cold water. She drew in the fresh, cool air as she stood at the outside bar.

She sensed his tall frame suddenly behind her without him even touching her, the heat emanating from his powerful body. She felt aroused and safe; protected and enticed; strangely familiar with his presence, despite having just exchanged a few sentences. She turned around to face him. Neither of them said a word. Their eyes did all the talking. Chaim put his hands on her hips and leaned in to kiss her. Sparkling rays of warmth radiated from his lips through her like an electric current. She lost herself in him. From that moment she was his. The power of his lips, his tongue, his body, his being completely overwhelmed her and swallowed her up. The enchanting voice of Texas' Spiteri singing *Put Your Arms Around Me* encapsulated them, making her feel like she was floating in a bubble with him, up, up and away.

They came up for air and became conscious of the world around them.

"Let's go," Chaim whispered in her ear.

She was not sure exactly how they got from the disco back to their kibbutz, but seemed to recall hitching a ride with some of his friends. She wondered how the old people got from the guest houses to the hot springs and snickered at the thought of them huddled up on the back of pickup trucks like migrant workers.

"What's so funny?" Chaim gave her a gentle squeeze then said a few words in Hebrew to his mates before opening the car door and letting them both out. Olivia continued giggling as they ran from the parking lot to the rows of little houses, her hand in his, never letting go.

Their panting broke the quiet darkness of his room. He scooped her up the second they stepped inside, her legs on each side of him, their mouths ravenously engaged in one eternal kiss. Up close his distinct Roman nose was surprisingly soft, giving in to the touch of hers, in contrast to his strong body. Their clothes soon landed on the floor. He put her down on his bed and climbed between her legs. He spread her fingers and caressed them with his. He placed his palms gently on hers then instantly pinned her hands to the mattress. His rough stubble brushed against her cheeks, then her breasts as his tongue travelled down her pounding body. She was bursting with new, mind-blowing sensations. Her whole being yearned for him, and all she could do was succumb, following his every lead. They both came loudly. He chuckled as he moved onto his back next to her.

"The guys next door are going to give me so much stick for this."

"What? Were we that loud?"

"Yes! And the walls are so thin it's ridiculous. But don't worry." He leaned over to kiss her crestfallen face. "I don't give a fuck, if you don't?" She laughed and rolled on top of him, caressing his chest. *This guy's a keeper.*

"Let's take a shower," he panted.

A shower? It was 2am and all she wanted to do was collapse into his arms and surrender to sleep. She did not want to break the magic spell, though, and followed him into the small bathroom where they cuddled and kissed under the tiny shower head till the hot water ran out. Then they fell asleep, naked, spent and clean, close together like two silver spoons in a velvet-clad drawer.

"What happened to you yesterday? Got us all worried disappearing into the night like that!" Charlie wore an uncharacteristically solemn expression when Olivia sat down at the breakfast table. *Now he's my father too?*

"I got a ride back with some of the local guys."

"Yeah, we figured that much!" Lola winked. Were they all her collective conscience all of a sudden?

"Someone called for you earlier. Daniel." Hannah was munching loudly on her toast.

Olivia's heart sank. *Shit.* She still had not called him and today was really not the best of days to do it. "Oh... Thanks. What did he say?"

"He just left a message for you to call him back when you get the chance."

Charlie's eyes caught hers. She swallowed and looked away. Who said life in a kibbutz was simple?

3

She could not believe it when she heard it on the radio. Naomi and Olivia had been dancing around the dining hall with their scrubbing brushes and floor wipers, singing along to Aqua's *Barbie Girl*. Olivia found it funny to hear the Danish band's catchy hit being broadcast so far away from home. The brief daily news in English came on, but the words sounded so alien.

"Princess Diana has died."

Olivia did not know her personally, of course, but she was such a public figure and someone she had followed and adored her entire childhood and teenage years, idolised in all her glory even after her scandalous divorce. Olivia felt she knew her from all the magazines and documentaries she had devoured with her grandmother, sharing their love of glamorous royals around the world. They were fascinated by Princess Diana in particular; her character so graceful and suffering; her life now ended so violently and abruptly. Everyone was surprised by the news, but no one in the kibbutz seemed to be affected in the same way as Olivia – not even Pippa and Bridget with their British heritage and love of history. Perhaps they mourned in their own way in private. She wondered if people around the world perceived the loss like she did. With her limited access to the media and current affairs it was difficult to decipher. She imagined the collective mourning: seas of flowers left by fans, notes of condolences by statesmen and commoners alike. Then she thought of the two little princes. The weight of the event was incomprehensible, exacerbated by Olivia and everyone around her just lulling along in their bubble of everyday life, protected from the world outside. She stared at her hands clutching the long handle of the floor brush, her movements suddenly lacking her usual energy. *I must call Grandma.* She carried the tragedy like a heavy rock in her stomach all day. It seemed like an omen in some strange way.

She had done the morning shift and finished early. She was surprised to see Charlie outside when she got back to their barracks.

"Hey, Liv. It's laundry day, yay!" He nodded at the big bag of clothes in front of him and the piles he had folded on the garden table. She noticed that his jesting words were not accompanied by the usual twinkle in his eyes. She smiled and joined him, sorting through the clothes. It was a weird, uncomfortable sensation having all your clothes jumbled together like this with those of people you hardly knew. She desperately searched for her underwear.

"Looking for these?" Charlie threw a pair of white lace knickers at her. Olivia caught them and quickly looked away.

His face was still solemn when she caught his eyes again.

"Did you hear about Princess Diana?" Olivia tried to break the awkward silence.

"Yes, I think the whole world knows, Liv."

She flinched.

"Sorry, I didn't mean to sneer at you. It's just… I got some bad news of my own I have to deal with, so can't really get worked up about a complete stranger passing away."

"Oh, I'm sorry... Do you want to talk about it?" She felt like a silly child, mourning the death of an idol like this. Seeing him upset suddenly made her feel guilty too for having pushed him away. Charlie sighed.

"My dad's not well, and my uncle needs me to step up, you know, to take over the family business. My mum keeps calling and writing... I've barely been away for a month!"

"Sounds like you have to go back... Before it's too late."

"Don't you think I know that?"

"Sorry, I just..."

"You just what, Liv? Wanted to state the obvious? That I really have no choice? Just like you, I want to be young and stupid while it's okay to be, and while I can. I want to run rampant and adventure and explore. I want to experience new things and new cultures and meet new people. But they can't even let me do that!" Charlie's voice broke and he looked away.

Olivia was shocked at his outburst; this big, noble guy unravelling before her eyes. But it was his words that stunned her the most. The realisation that she too was here on borrowed time. That in only a few months she would have to step out of the exotic fairy tale bubble in which they were all frolicking and return to reality. A reality designed by others, based on the expectations of her family and society that she would return to the predicted path of university, career, marriage and motherhood – all in the safe confines of her upper class life. She had been allowed to steer off the path, but only temporarily. Just like Charlie.

She leaned over and gave his hand a squeeze. They looked into each other's eyes and both knew. They were the same, yet different. Olivia's journey of self-discovery had just begun and who knew where it would take her and for how long it would last. But for Charlie it was coming to an end already.

He suddenly cupped her face between his hands.

"Come with me, Olivia, back to Oxford. Help me make this life an adventure – not a prison of conformity and, and… predictability!" His eyes sparkled and his playful smile had returned.

Olivia tittered and moved his hands gently. He held on to hers. She was surprised by his spontaneous offer and struggled to take it seriously.

"I can't, Charlie."

"Why not?" His newfound excitement was contagious, but she did not want to lead him on any longer than neces-sary – especially as he now looked like he genuinely meant that she was to abandon everything to come and live with him. They hardly knew each other!

"Because…" She smiled shyly and trailed off. There were so many reasons.

"Because of that guy back home you never call?"

Olivia sniffed and frowned. "No…" How was he able to see right through her like this? There was a pause before Charlie added two and two together.

"Because of Mango Boy?" Charlie looked her straight in the eye. "Oh my god, Liv, you've fallen for Mango Boy!" He guffawed. Olivia gritted her teeth and let go of Charlie's hands.

"I don't expect you to understand…"

"Oh, I understand, Liv. He's everything your guy back home isn't. But don't you see it can never be more than a fling? A random piece in your puzzle of rebellion?"

The resentment was boiling inside her. How dared he judge her and label her like that?

"Just stop, Charlie. You don't know anything about him and how this is going to turn out."

"Maybe I don't know him, but I know you, and…"

"No, Charlie! You keep saying that, but actually you don't know me. You've just met me. Yes, we may come from the same kind of background. Yes, we may be headed in a similar direction in life. And it may for some reason be bloody obvious to everybody despite all my attempts to avoid it. But I am not going to let you pigeonhole me like everyone else into anything! Let me have my adventure. Let me carve my own path. And yes, let me fall in love with whomever I want. Because that's my right! And face it, Charlie, we may have a connection, but I am not in love with you!"

Charlie pulled back. His eyes narrowed to two dark incisions and flickered across Olivia's face, his body suddenly tense and his breathing suspended for a brief moment. They were both frozen in time. She could hear her own breath, rapid and burning in her throat as she bit the inside of her cheek. Her eyes broke away from Charlie's.

"Wow! Well, now we've got that straight, I think I'll just go and pack my bag." He grabbed his folded laundry and stormed into his room.

Olivia slumped back in the garden chair and buried her face in her hands.

"What's the deal with that Charlie guy?" Chaim rested his head on his folded arms. They were making out in his room, entangled on the bed. Olivia had gone straight off to find him after showering and getting changed. Every cell of her body was screaming to be with him.

Olivia frowned. "What do you mean?"

"He's very… focused on you." Chaim stroked her arm.

"Well, I'm not into him if that's what you're worried about." She thought of her argument with Charlie that afternoon.

"Hmm." His face did not give anything away. "Rumours tell another story."

She pulled herself up to sitting. "What rumours?"

He had that serious look on him now – the soldier face.

"Have you been with him?"

"What? No!" What did that even mean – been with him?

Chaim eyed her suspiciously. Olivia swallowed.

"He kissed me once. On my first day here. It was nothing…"

His gaze pierced into her – those intense brown eyes mastered so many contrasting emotions: affection, lust, reproach, anger… She shifted, pulling the stray strap of her top back up on her bare shoulders. Her ears were burning and her insides turning. Her good girl label had certainly been torn off.

"And that's all?"

Should she seize the awkward moment and tell him? She wet her lips.

"Back home…"

There was a knock on the door. Chaim called out: "*Ken?*"

Despite the positive acknowledgement, she could hear the irritation in his voice. She exhaled and closed her eyes when his friend, Tomer, entered. Daniel was still safe in the closet. For now.

"It's so good to hear your voice!"

Olivia cleared her throat. Daniel's voice sounded foreign to her. She struggled to match his affection and excitement at finally talking to each other again.

"How are you? Have you made some new army friends?" Her upbeat tone was absurdly forced. She rolled her eyes at herself.

"Good, good. Yes, they're a fun bunch. Quite pleasant – most of them. And you? Are people nice to you?"

"Yes, they're all lovely." She instantly pictured Chaim and his enigmatic eyes, his chiselled cheekbones and every bit of his body so ridiculously beautiful. Olivia twisted the hem of her skirt around her finger. Her mind desperately tried to refocus on Daniel and to come up with something relevant to say to him.

"I miss you." Daniel's words cut through her daydreaming.

What was she supposed to say? That she did not miss him? That she did not love him anymore? That she had moved on to new adventures the moment she had left Denmark? That to her own great surprise she did not regret a single thing? That she could no longer in her wildest dreams imagine herself living a life with him? Because her wildest dreams now centred around one person only: Chaim.

"How are your parents?" Olivia's random response to his heartfelt declaration was met with silence.

"They're fine, thank you." Daniel sounded colder now. "My mother worries about me. About us. Your mother does too, I've gathered."

Olivia's throat tightened. She was suffocating at the thought of their two mothers gossiping and scheming at their ladies' lunches and garden parties. She did not belong in their inbred circle of life. She refused. She managed to cut their conversation short with a promise to call again soon. She could breathe anew. Her conscience was clear. For the moment.

That Friday was Charlie's last in the kibbutz. The volunteers had all pitched in to throw him an improvised leaving party at the leisure activity room set up in one of the safety bunkers.

At dinner, Olivia once more wondered about the socialist kibbutz honouring the *Shabbat* with *challah* – the braided white bread with sesame seeds which she found delicious. She knew there were a few religious kibbutzim in Israel, but this was not one of them. Naomi had told her it was mainly to keep the old people in the guest houses happy. The kibbutz emphasised the connection to nature and the land, rather than a god, in their celebrations. Olivia came to the conclusion that religion was just as much a basis for cultural norms and culinary traditions here as it was in her home country. You did not have to be religious to eat eggs and lamb for Easter or sugary pastry for Lent. Nor did any of her friends think twice about why their day of rest was Sunday or the true reasons for celebrating Christmas. It was just part of their everyday life.

They all felt gutted that Charlie was leaving – including Olivia, despite their complicated, short-lived relationship. He was the life of their continuous party – always ready with a joke, a smile and a cuddle; his energy and laughter so contagious. Olivia seemed to be the only one to know that although all of this was genuine, it was still a desperate attempt at squeezing everything he could out of his adventures here before surrendering to his fate: a life which had been chosen for him as managing director for a major steel conglomerate.

Olivia fiddled with the label of her beer as she watched the other volunteers play pool at the table in the middle of the room, some laughing and some singing along to the tunes from the small portable radio.

"A penny for your thoughts?" Charlie sidled up and nudged her shoulder with his.

She smiled. She was pleasantly surprised that he had approached her as they had not talked since that afternoon.

"Just wondering what it will be like here without you."

"Well, you're not going to miss me, that's for sure." His wry tone revealed he was still hurt.

"Come on, Charlie, don't be like that," she sighed. "It's your last night here and everyone's come to party with you – including me. I'm really sorry for the way things worked out the other day, but I don't want to end it all like this."

"Like what? Me offering you a fabulous life and you rejecting me without batting an eyelid?"

She could tell he was not used to rejection and she still felt guilty, but what was she supposed to do? She had her own ambitions and plans to pursue. And her feelings for Chaim were increasingly beyond her control.

"Charlie, you are a fantastic guy."

Charlie scoffed and rolled his eyes. "Clearly not fantastic enough for you."

"Just let me finish. I'm sure you will find a fantastic girl who can challenge you and join you on all your adventures…"

"What adventures? My life is over now." His hands made a dramatic gesture.

"Seriously, Charlie – would you rather have to risk your life like the guys here have to? Think about how lucky you are. You never have to worry about money or enemies or fighting for your life for real."

"Nope. All I have to do is carry the legacy of three generations on my shoulders and try not to fuck it all up." He took a large swig of his bottle.

She realised then that he was scared. He was not just a young philanderer frustrated by having to miss out on the fun – he was a little boy frightened by the responsibilities and expectations he now had to face every day for the rest of his life. Olivia put her bottle down and pulled him in for a hug. He put his arms around her and held her so tight she thought he was never going to let go. He still smelt so nice. *Lovely Charlie.* She became aware of the others looking at them and tried to wriggle away. His one arm stayed around her lower back, his other lifted to caress her hair.

"Are you sure I can't tempt you to come with me?"

She laughed. He would do just fine in the corporate world of strong-arming bullies.

"I'm sure."

"Feel free to visit me anytime." He wriggled his eyebrows.

"Thanks, Charlie," she chuckled. "Now let's join the others and have some serious fun!"

"I won't say no to that!"

The alcohol kept flowing and as their sound levels rose, some locals popped in and joined their party, including the life guard guy and a few of the soldiers living in the barracks behind the volunteers. The soldiers were an integral part of the kibbutz, staying close to where they were stationed, but far from their families. Olivia struck up a conversation with one of them, Uri. After a few beers he got quite agitated and started vividly explaining why he was willing to sacrifice his life to defend his country, and his innate hatred of Palestinians.

"We are the persecuted people! The Territories are not occupied – we liberated the land. Our land!"

"So all those people in the Gaza Strip and West Bank, trying to go about their lives in peace – are you saying they're not oppressed?" Bridget ventured.

"You of all people should know then what it feels like to be living in constant fear and pain," Olivia said, attempting to encourage empathy. Uri turned his head sharply and gave her a harsh squint. Olivia was taken aback and struggled to understand. How could someone seemingly normal be born and raised to hate other human beings? No history lesson could have prepared her for this cultural encounter.

"None of you know anything about how it feels to be an Israeli!" Uri hissed.

"You think you're the only one to grow up in a split country? You think you're the only one who knows what it's like to have enemies on your doorstep? I grew up with bombs in the street and strict curfews and people dying round me too. But you don't see me spreading hate like a bloody crusader, do you?"

Olivia was surprised when the usually quiet Aidan suddenly pitched in on the lively discussion. Uri got to his feet and gave Aidan a forceful push to the chest.

"So you think you're better than me, huh?"

"Yeah, as a matter of fact I do, you feckin eejit!" Aidan pushed him back. Olivia got up and tried to stop them.

"Come on, guys..."

The enraged soldier pushed her away so hard that she fell onto a nearby sofa. Out of nowhere a tall, dark guy intervened and punched Uri in the face. He stumbled onto the pool table. The room fell silent, bar the music on the radio and a few gasps from the crowd. Her defender turned around as he shook his fist loose – it was Chaim! She had never seen anyone fight in real life. She looked down at the few blood stains which had sprayed onto her top from Uri's lips and nose. She started shaking. This was nothing like on film. This was someone's blood on her. She looked at Chaim and could feel her tears welling up. She was relieved and proud that he had come to her rescue, but his brute force scared her too. She had never met anyone like him. He was a born soldier. He rushed to her and held her, searching her eyes.

"Are you okay?"

She nodded, but was still shaking and out of words. He kissed her forehead, gave her a big, gentle squeeze, then started guiding her out of the room.

"Come on, let's get you out of here."

She turned her head as she walked out the door and caught Charlie's eyes. He mouthed "Goodbye".

4

I t was quieter in the kibbutz after Charlie left. Less interaction among the volunteers at least. Hannah and Lola integrated well with the kitchen staff. Hannah in particular struck up a friendship with one of the older women, Vardit. This feisty little woman often bossed Olivia around and told her off for the slightest things. Olivia wondered why, but brushed it off.

She built her own relationships with Naomi, as well as Chaim's friends, and focused on learning the local culture and language from them. It was such a challenge for her not knowing the alphabet. She could not read the newspapers, billboards or back of milk cartons. She was dependent on others teaching her every word; through popular songs and TV series; the food they ate, the drinks they shared; their jokes, banter and general conversations.

Her new, local friends were of the last generation to have lived in the children's house – essentially a socialist construction which allowed their parents to focus on working for the greater good of the kibbutz and mainly spend time with their children during meal times and other family activities. This communal child-rearing method meant that everything from food and sleep to clothing, hygiene and medical treatment was the responsibility of not the parents, but this collective education authority. Although the concept seemed foreign to the volunteers, it had forged strong bonds between the young people of this generation; young people who also shared the looming, life-changing event of having to enter the Israeli army. Their future roles were still unknown, but the general risks entailed were obvious. It was a very different ballgame to that of the adolescent soldiers of peaceful Denmark who at this point in time had no natural opponents or impending dangers lurking on their diplomatic doorstep. Danish soldiers were increasingly involved in NATO and UN operations, including the Gulf and Bosnian Wars, but on a voluntary basis. Her own Daniel had been drafted and was eagerly taking part in the mandatory training for hypothetical what-ifs – in stark contrast to her new friends who would be trained to kill for survival.

It was an alien feeling to live in a country with so many enemies; always some degree of imminent risk hanging over their heads. Life in the kibbutz was like living in a bubble, though, sheltered from the troubles outside, many originating only a few miles away in the Gaza Strip. The young kibbutzniks – boys and girls alike – preparing for the army, as well as the omnipresent green-clad soldiers on buses, street corners and fast food restaurants were a constant reminder of the dangers rippling under the surface. Olivia had been concerned, of course, before leaving for this troubled country. Watching horrific images of the aftermath of recent suicide bombs on the news did not help. But reports from friends of friends returning from fantastic kibbutz stays kept her worries at ease and fed her determination to explore this to her unknown country; a country which seemed to have everything – sea, mountains, deserts and oases – except peace.

"How can someone hate so much – and a whole people they don't even know?" Olivia had been trying to process what had happened with the soldier, Uri, the night of the party in the bunker. She needed to know that Chaim was different.

Chaim put a lock of hair behind her ear and sighed. "You have to understand what our people have been through. We have a long history of being the victims."

"So that gives you the right to bully others into becoming victims too?"

He sat up on the bed, his lips now pressed tightly. "I don't expect you to understand…"

"But I want to understand!" Olivia interrupted him. She grabbed his hands. "I really do."

He looked into her pleading eyes for a moment then smiled.

"Okay. Well, how much do you know about Israel's history?" He clasped his hands.

"I know the highlights. From school and the media."

"The media, huh," Chaim snorted.

Olivia had grown up during the years of the intifada and the Oslo peace process, but only following it all from afar, of course; seeing it through the eyes of a child trying to understand the world. Sound bites and images from the news were jumbled in her mind, making it difficult to determine right from wrong and the facts of history. She was well-read and old enough now to know that those facts depended on the eyes of the beholder – the victors versus the conquered. Nothing was objective.

Olivia deduced that Chaim's parents had done their best to instil in him a balanced view of the world and his immediate surroundings. However, the influence of school – teachers and peers alike – friends, group pressure, the hungry media and persuasive propaganda, all vying for your attention, was hard to avoid when forming your own opinion as a young person. Olivia knew that all too well, although the issues she had struggled with were of a different nature. She listened intently as Chaim talked her through his version of history: Israel's victories and defeats; peace talks and breakdowns; and when it had all gone awry, in general leaving the Israelis to be as hated in many places as the Arabs were by the Israelis; the sound of the sirens in a child's ears, running to safety in a bunker, his mother and father holding his hands, whispering words of comfort as his innocent heart was thumping in his little chest; the dusty streets of Gaza and children hiding behind piles of rubbish; uncles lost in fighting, cousins without fathers; demonstrators and terrorists; bombings and killings; the vile smell of gas masks and the sweet taste of freedom. Olivia pressed her hands against her stomach, shaking her head, processing everything.

"I don't share this hatred, Liv." His voice was soft now. He could read the worry in her eyes. She had been quiet for a long time, taking it all in. She bit her lip. He leant forward and drew circles on her arm with his large, but gentle fingers.

"I don't want to be that soldier beating up Palestinians with my rifle, stomping my army boots all over people's homes and lives." Olivia flinched at the graphic image he conjured. She did not want him to be that person either.

"I will do my best to be fair. To be a human." He swallowed. "But things will get messy. And I have a job to do when I get out there."

"I know." Olivia looked down at her hands, picking at her cuticles. Her chest was heavy all of a sudden.

"Hey, don't worry." Chaim lifted her chin gently and held her gaze. "I will be back before you know it, and I will still be the same guy sitting here craving to kiss you and explore every part of you."

She threw her head back, laughing out loud – with relief and appreciation. He chuckled and tumbled upon her, nibbling her ear. She shrieked, but gave in to his playful kisses, unable to escape from under his heavy body – and not wanting to either.

A highlight of the week was receiving mail from home or her travelling friends. She would check the volunteers' allocated space in the rows of wooden pigeonholes along the wall of the communal entrance hall when she left work every day. Letters from her grandmother were always received with a warm heart and slight tears in her eyes; recounting pieces from her daily life and bits of local news, completed with caring words of affection, not once mentioning her illness.

A stamp from France would mean a letter from Amalie, her oldest friend, who was studying in Paris. She had been shocked and disappointed when Olivia had decided she was not joining her, ditching her in favour of "some semi-socialist quest into a war zone" as Amalie had described it. Nevertheless, it seemed like Amalie enjoyed Olivia's colourful accounts of her adventures in their mail correspondence. Olivia found that she did not envy Amalie's life of continuous pub crawls, clothes shopping and amorous escapades topped up with dragging lectures and tedious tests – to her own surprise. She had not written to Amalie – or anyone back home – about Chaim. She was not ready to let her two worlds merge just yet, nor for the consequences this would have.

She spent every waking hour she could – and the sleeping ones too – with Chaim.

She would hang out with Naomi and a few other local girls after work, chatting in staccato Hebrew-English, keen to belong, as she watched Chaim play basketball with his mates on the warm tarmac behind one of the barns, his shots never missing the worn out hoop. He had been a star player on his school team according to Tomer. She did not doubt it for one moment looking at his tall, athletic body manoeuvring the other players and handling the ball with incredible ease and gracefulness. Game over successfully, Chaim strode across the court beaming at her. He took off his cap and wiped his face with his T-shirt before he bent down to kiss her. She stretched up on her toes and tilted her head back to welcome his panting mouth with equal measures pride and excitement as she sensed the eyes of the other girls upon them. He was hers, and she was his.

Chaim worked till late on the last day of the cotton harvest. Olivia had gone to his room to wait for him and fallen asleep. She heard the door open far away beyond her dreams. He sidled up to her from behind, nuzzling her neck. She could smell his clean, soapy smell even underneath a long day's work. His hand travelled up under her T-shirt and cupped her breast firmly.

"Mmm… I'm sleeping," she moaned, amusement playing on her lips.

"That's okay. Keep sleeping. This is just a dream. A very wet dream."

She smiled and rolled over to face him, her eyes still closed. She kissed him and his tongue soon found hers. She arched her back as he slid her panties off with his capable hands, then welcomed him inside her with a gasp of pleasure. She never tired of his touch, tender yet strong, and the rhythm of his movements always in tune with hers. She climbed on top and rode him till they both came, collapsing in each other's arms. *Sweet dreams indeed.*

She hardly noticed him sliding out of bed and into the bathroom as she dozed off to the faint sound of the shower. *The cleanest man on the planet,* she smiled in her sleep.

It was Lola's crazy idea, but the other volunteers had run with it without hesitation, excited and desperate for an adventure to break up the monotony of their everyday lives in the kibbutz. They were going to take the bus into Ashqelon straight after work on the Friday afternoon, swim in the sea and camp on the beach to sleep under the stars. There were no late buses back to the kibbutz anyway, so their only options were to hitchhike or sleep there till morning. Chaim was less thrilled about the plan.

"The beach is not safe at night. All kinds of types hang out there."

"Don't worry – Aidan and James will be there too."

"Huh." His head gave a small disapproving jerk.

"It will be fine." She laughed and kissed his frowning forehead.

It was a welcome respite for them all to be away from the kibbutz. It was a lovely and safe environment, but small and suffocating too – especially for a group of young people who had ventured out to see the world. They squealed and cheered as they ran into the waves, splashing about ecstatically. The sea cleansed and energised them, making them feel like the kids they all were inside. They were laughing and chatting loudly, trying to build primitive drying racks for their wet towels and laying out their spartan dinner provisions, when she saw them coming over the grey dunes. She quickly recognised their broad, agile frames against the dusky background. Chaim was nearly a head taller than his friends, Tomer and Ben. Tomer's dark blonde hair always puzzled her – so different to his peers. She wondered where he originated from. Everyone was from somewhere. Olivia loved discovering people's stories, and they were plentiful in these foreign surroundings.

"Hi!" she shouted and waved, then ran up the dunes to greet them. "What a nice surprise! What are you doing here?"

"Just thought I would check in on you." A flicker of wariness ran across Chaim's smiling face as he bent down to kiss her.

"I'm so happy you did. You can come and help us with the fire. We can't seem to get it started properly." She grabbed his hand and pulled him down to their improvised camp.

The three soldiers-in-waiting soon got the fire roaring. A huge log was burning, one end sticking far out into the sand.

"That will keep you warm through the night." Tomer brushed the dirt off his palms with satisfied claps. "You just have to keep moving it further into the fire when it burns."

Aidan and James gave the kibbutzniks an approving nod and threw them each a can of beer.

"Don't lie too close to it." Chaim moved Olivia's sleeping bag away from the fire. "Don't want you to wake up in flames."

She beamed at him and kissed his cheek. They all sat around the fire, chatting, singing, drinking beer. Olivia tried to capture the magical moment with her camera.

She had never felt so free and careless before. The stars twinkling above; her head resting on Chaim's shoulder; his hand caressing her hair. Weightless and happy she floated into the night.

She woke up with the sun on her face, boiling in her sleeping bag. The flies had bothered her for hours now, but she had managed to keep dozing back off. Chaim and his friends had left in their car just after midnight. She had stayed with the other volunteers, determined to enjoy the full outdoors nocturnal experience, despite Chaim's attempts to persuade her to come back to the kibbutz with him.

"*At bahurah akshanit* – you stubborn girl." He had shaken his head, then smiled and kissed her goodnight.

She rubbed a hand over her eyes and grimaced. Her head was pounding, and she could feel the sand everywhere, including between her gritted teeth. She sat up and searched for a bottle of water. She glanced at her watch. Not even 7am. Despite the surprising strength of the sun at this time of day, there was a misty haze across the sky. She desperately wanted to run into the sea and rinse off the smell of smoke and the clammy feeling of cold sweat. The others stirred.

As their little camp came to life again, they shared some fruit and bread then started packing their things. They enjoyed the sun and the sea for a couple of hours before the haze thickened. The wind increased in strength and suddenly a wall of thick, indefinable matter appeared to be coming closer and closer.

"It's a sandstorm!" James shouted.

They all grabbed their belongings, and as the blanket of whirling sand grains built up, grazing their skin and irritating their eyes, they ran away from the beach towards the main road to seek shelter. Pippa tripped and fell. Olivia bent down and grabbed her hand to pull her up, but was startled by Pippa's scream.

"My foot!"

Pippa struggled to stand. Olivia called out to the others who were halfway to the bus stop already. She managed to prop up Pippa's plump frame as she started hobbling along. They were saved by Aidan who rushed to support Pippa's other side.

"What's happened?" His Irish sing-song was rarely heard. A man of few, but usually kind, words.

"I think I twisted my ankle. Running is not really my forte." Pippa attempted a shy, apologetic smile.

"How bad is it?" Aidan kneeled down to inspect the damage. Pippa pulled her foot away then grimaced from the rapid movement.

"Easy now." Aidan looked up at her, his calm eyes disarming. "Maybe a trip to A&E?"

"No, no, don't be silly." Pippa brushed him off and attempted to walk on her own. She fell into Olivia's arms after one unsuccessful step. Olivia's mind was spinning its cogs by now. Where was the nearest hospital? What would the standard of doctors and treatments be? Was it even clean and safe? She realised these thoughts were likely to be running through Pippa's mind too. Olivia effaced her frown and gave her new friend an encouraging smile.

"Don't you think it's best if you just get it checked over?"

"I'm not sure my insurance will cover it." Pippa's voice was even feebler than usual as she looked at the ground.

Olivia had not thought about any cost. In Denmark, health care was free for all. Well, nothing was free in life, of course. The welfare state was funded by the high taxes her parents moaned about. She had taken out travel insurance on her father's insistence while planning her exotic adventures. At the time she had thought of theft and damages as the main risks she would encounter. She had probably been in denial about potential bodily injuries.

The sand was getting everywhere now. The hobbling trio kept their heads down and made it to the bus stop where they filled in the others on the situation.

"There's a hospital here in town. The kibbutz office mentioned it once." Bridget gave Pippa's shoulder a squeeze.

"You have to go no matter what. You can't walk around in pain like that." Olivia frowned. "We'll all pitch in if the cost becomes an issue."

The others jerked their heads and stared at Olivia. *Or maybe not.* Olivia turned her back and hailed the first taxi she spotted. Aidan helped Pippa into the backseat where Olivia joined her. Their fellow volunteers waved goodbye, their faces sheepish in the shadow of the bus shelter.

The local hospital looked just like any other Olivia had encountered back home. The service was swift and the treatment efficient. She winced at her previous doubts. She still knew so little of her host country. She was grateful for another experience to widen her horizon – although Pippa probably did not see it quite the same way.

Most of the staff spoke English and helped the girls figure out the whole payment question. Pippa's basic travel insurance covered the consultation, X-ray and expert bandaging of her sprained ankle. She was even supplied with a pair of crutches before the girls made their way back to the kibbutz; their fun seaside adventure a distant memory as they struggled from bus to bus and finally up the long path to their barracks.

"I told you the beach was a dangerous place." Relief fought with blame in Chaim's voice. He was waiting on Olivia's front step and leaped up the moment he saw her. Pippa the Patient hugged and thanked her before retreating, welcomed back by Bridget's open arms.

"Man, I was so worried about you. When the others came back without you and they said you were at the hospital…" Chaim shook his head and pulled Olivia in for a big cuddle.

"I'm absolutely fine," she murmured into his broad chest. She felt her body relax in his arms, only just realising how tense she had been all day. She looked up at Chaim with a tired smile. Their lips met in a tender kiss as dusk fell upon them. For the first time Olivia felt at home.

Life in the kibbutz went on in the same groove, only interrupted by a few extraordinary events like the celebrations
of *Rosh Hashana* – the Jewish New Year. Apples dipped in
honey, symbolising a sweet year, and bountiful pomegran-
ates with their many seeds were enjoyed by all. *Yom Kippur*
followed soon after. The Day of Atonement was the holiest
day of the year in Judaism, Olivia had read, completing
the *Yamim Nora'im* – the High Holy Days commencing with
Rosh Hashanah. According to tradition, each person's fate
for the coming year were inscribed into the Book of Life by
God on Rosh Hashanah, but he waited until Yom Kippur
to seal the verdict. No religious ceremonies took place in
the kibbutz, though. The *shofar* was blown on the eve of
the New Year as a symbolic gesture, but no one prayed and
no one fasted during these beautiful October days. They
threw a New Year's barbecue instead and got the day off
on both occasions – to the volunteers' great enjoyment.
The words of Yom Kippur rang a bell in Olivia's mental
history records and their sombre connotations made her
less inclined to party. The memory of images of a dirty
war, although it took place years before she was born, induced an inclination to reflect instead; about her own life
and history and how it was suddenly intertwined with that
of a country, culture and people so different and far away
from home; about the grittiness and gore of war which she
still struggled to fathom.

It got colder at night. The volunteers were advised to check
their shoes and sleeping bags for snakes and scorpions

which would stray inside at this time of year. The mornings were crisp, and the sun took longer to warm up the air.

Olivia overcame her apprehensions and ventured to the hot springs with Bridget and Pippa. However, the overpowering smell of rotten eggs made it impossible for her to enjoy the healing powers of the warm water. The smell lingered on her skin for days after. She never went back.

The Danish trio joked about how their English had both improved and worsened; their vocabulary expanded thanks to their British peers, but their grammar and accents were confused by speaking a mixture of languages with their local colleagues. They had even started dreaming in broken English as opposed to their native tongue. Olivia wondered what it would be like to be back home again, not just surrounded by people speaking Danish, but also submerged in the well-known humdrum of everyday life and a familiar environment.

Each day added to Olivia's cultural experiences and Middle Eastern adventures in some way or another. Each day subtracted from the time she had left with Chaim. Each day she fell more in love and dreaded the inevitable day she would have to say goodbye to her beloved. The closer they got to both their scheduled departures, the more creative the ideas in her head became for how to continue their lives together, otherwise destined for different paths entirely. Perhaps she could find a relevant job in town for a while; become a translator or a teacher; work at the airline or the embassy or… She never voiced them, though, wary of spoiling their precious time together.

"My little Liv! How is your great adventure?" Her grandmother's voice sounded frail, but cheerful.

"Oh, Grandma, it's magical! Everything I dreamed of and much more." Olivia was bursting to tell her about Chaim. She had shared every secret with her grandmother since she could remember. Yet she hesitated.

"Any dragons to slay? Or maybe some handsome princes rescuing beautiful princesses?"

"You know I don't need any rescuing, Grandma." Olivia tittered.

"I know, my dear. But sometimes our hearts take us down paths we do not expect…" A loaded silence passed. Olivia cleared her throat and tucked her hair behind her ear.

"How are you feeling? Got your energy back for beating those girlfriends of yours in bridge again?"

"Not yet, my dear. But I will return with bells on, and they won't know what hit them."

"I'm sure you will," Olivia laughed and her grandmother joined in, but was soon halted by a chesty cough.

"Are you sure you're okay?" Olivia furrowed her brows.

"Yes, yes, don't you worry about me. I just got a little something tickling my throat. I'd better go get some water."

"Well, you take care now."

"I'm not the one slaying dragons. You focus on your wonderful quest, and I will be right here waiting to hear all about it."

"I'll call and write soon again." She longed to give her grandmother a hug.

"Whenever you have the time, my dear."

A shiver ran through her as she hung up. She paused with her hand on the receiver, but was interrupted in her thoughts by Vardit calling her name from the kitchen. Her brief break was over.

The volunteers swam in the pool most afternoons till it closed when the weather during the day got cooler too.

Lola had built up a crush on the life guard, Itai, and took every chance she could to engage and flirt with him – intensifying her efforts now that she knew he was moving on to other pastures soon. He had often joined them for a game of pool at the bunker, but he never seemed to recip-rocate Lola's advances – to her great frustration.

When Olivia mentioned it to Chaim one day he chortled.

"Don't you know? He's gay!"

"No way!" He seemed so macho. She analysed her mem-ory for any giveaways. Perhaps he was a bit more groomed and self-conscious than other guys in the kibbutz? She con-cluded that he was just a guy like any other – who happened to not be romantically interested in Lola or any girls. *I really have to get all those stereotypes out of my head!*

"Well, that explains it." She thought about how to share this information with Lola in the least humiliating and heart-breaking way.

"Even if he wasn't, he would probably run away screaming."

"What do you mean?" Lola was an attractive girl with her slender frame and long, blondish hair.

"You know… She's a bit of a… She tries too hard, let me put it that way."

"Are you saying my friend is a slut?"

He shrugged with a sly smile. "I don't think so, of course, but the guys talk…"

"And what do they say about me then?"

"They don't dare say anything about you, because you're mine." He pulled her in and bit her neck playfully. Olivia squealed and surrendered to his strong hold and enticing kisses.

She savoured their evenings together; cuddling up on his bed, watching TV, asking him to translate the news, commercials, scenes and dialogue that made him laugh or swear. And then there was Bamba – the national snack. Little peanut butter-flavoured puffs that even came in giant bags. Olivia could devour a whole bowl in minutes, leaving her utterly content, her belly blowing defiant raspberries at her mother's reprimanding voice at the back of her mind.

"I've become totally addicted to these!"

"I've noticed!" Chaim chuckled. "And I've become to-tally addicted to you!" He rolled on top of her and tasted her lips. "Bamba monster."

She laughed. "Hey, who's the monster here?"

She loved the feeling of his powerful body between her legs. She slipped her hands under his ragged, white T-shirt, then let them glide across his toned chest. Desire was burning in his eyes. She could feel him pounding through his worn-out jeans. Her hands travelled to grab his flexing buttocks and they met in a ravenous kiss. She gave in to her primal instincts, her urge to be one with him overruling everything.

"You're using too much soap again."

Olivia looked up from the brown and white marbled tiles at Vardit's sullen face. She was using the exact amount of soap Naomi had shown her and always used herself when washing the floors.

"You will need too much water to rinse it off. It's a waste."

Olivia sighed. The whole process was ridiculously time and resource consuming to begin with. First pouring out the scoops of thick green soap in strategic places across the vast dining hall floor; then flooding it entirely with water from a hose; followed by scrubbing it till your hands hurt. Next ensued the eternal dance of manoeuvring the masses of water with a giant floor scraper into the narrow gratings at each end of the hall; one by the side entrance door where you could steal a breath of fresh air, gazing at the greenery outside; and one in the hot and humid room where dishes were scraped into huge bins and placed onto the racks of the conveyor belt leading into the industrial dishwasher. This was also where Olivia encountered cockroaches for the first time in her life.

By the time Olivia was done with the Sisyphean task, her clothes were drenched in sweat and she was panting from exhaustion. *What happened to a good old-fashioned mop and bucket?* That seemed sufficient for the cleaners at her parents' large house, which was always pristine. At least the girls only had to wash the floors twice per week in the kibbutz – the other days they swept them with a broom – and Olivia could rest in the knowledge that the place in which she ate her meals was completely clean.

She had done the early morning shift, followed by the late afternoon one today. She was too tired to argue with Vardit. She really did not understand how Hannah had become friends with such an enervating grouch. What did they have in common? She often wondered what they joked about when she heard them cackling in the kitchen. The biggest mystery, however, was what this woman had against Olivia. She could not think of one thing she could have done to ruffle her feathers.

Olivia rolled her eyes inwardly and kept silent as she returned to scrubbing the floors, her back turned to her constant critic. Vardit mumbled something in Hebrew under her breath then turned and left her to it. *M'funeket* was the only word Olivia caught from the muffled tirade. She tossed it in her head for the rest of the afternoon, not wanting to ask Naomi what it meant when her friend rejoined her after finishing the toilets downstairs.

"It means spoiled. Like in spoiled brat," Chaim explained to her that evening. She was cuddling up in the nook of his muscular arm, her head resting on his chest. She sensed it rising and descending at a peaceful pace. She turned her head and frowned at him.

"Why would she call me that? She doesn't even know me!" Olivia felt a knot in her stomach. "I do all my tasks exactly as and when I'm required to. I never complain. I…" She trailed off. She really did not understand it. Chaim stroked her bare arm gently and kissed the top of her head.

"Some kibbutzniks just don't like foreign volunteers. My mother is the same. Or can be. Not always," he quickly interjected. "Don't worry about it. Vardit has always been a grumpy old fart, but she's not a bad person. From what my mother has told me, she's had a tough life. Maybe that just makes her bitter at the world."

"Huh." Olivia reflected. She logged the chance snippet of information about his mother in the back of her mind, mentally muting the tiny alarm bell that had gone off with it. "She doesn't seem very bitter and unfriendly around the other girls in the kitchen, though."

"Maybe she's jealous of your grace and good looks." Chaim smiled.

Olivia scoffed and gave him a nudge. "Now you're just teasing me." It would not be the first time someone held her status and good fortune against her. But no one in the kibbutz really knew her background, except maybe from Chaim who must have gathered bits and pieces by now. That was the whole point of coming here in the first place: a fresh start; trying on a different identity; getting to know her true self beneath all the superficial layers of status and expectations. Was she really that transparent? She recalled Charlie's apposite remarks during her first week here. His characterisation of her had been unnerving, yet accurate. It seemed like a lifetime ago already. She wondered how he was getting on with his responsibilities back in England. Chaim cut through her momentary reveries.

"Well, I'm not going to complain about your looks. In fact, let me just check you out again." He pulled the blanket aside and ran both his hands down the sides of her body, kneeling at her feet. Olivia yelped as the cool air hit her naked body.

"Nope. No complaints." He winked and flashed a cheeky grin.

She giggled and soon gave in to his gentle, but firm, caresses with an ecstatic moan. She raised her hips, her body open and welcoming, as he found his way between her thighs with confidence and ease. She could not get enough of him.

Olivia and Chaim walked along the fields one early evening, meandering in the sunset, holding hands and exchanging stories. She ran her fingers through the tall grass bordering the rows of now naked cotton plants.

"My dad's a law professor at the university. My mother owns a law firm." She decided to omit the size of the firm. As their relationship had developed, she was eager to tell Chaim about herself, but still worried how he would react if she told him that the headcount of her mother's company was as large as the population of the kibbutz.

"They met as students in the seventies – law, of course. My dad was doing an international law course in Paris for a semester, and he somehow swept my mother off her feet and convinced her to come back with him to Copenhagen. She's probably regretted it ever since..."

"What makes you say that?"

She shrugged. "She's just so cold and bitter all the time."

"Would it be better if they divorced like mine?"

Olivia could not imagine her parents not being together. They had a deep respect for one another. And the love was still there somewhere, she sensed. Just not the explicit kind.

"Why did your parents split up?" she deflected.

Chaim let out a scoffing laugh. "My dad couldn't keep it in his pants."

"Oh!" Olivia thought of the nice, middle-aged man with the grey hair and well-padded physique to whom Chaim had introduced her haphazardly at lunch one day.

"I know – he may not look the part, but he's a stealth Casanova!"

Olivia chuckled. "So they both still live in the kibbutz?" She had not had a chance to meet his mother yet.

"Yeah. My mom mostly keeps to herself. Works at the library." He picked up a stone and threw it away from the fields. A small lizard scurried away from where it landed.

Olivia was of the impression that Jewish boys had solid relationships with their mothers, but of course that was another stereotype from films she had to dismiss from her skewed understanding of the world. She gave her head a little shake at the thought of her own naivety and how limited her life had been so far despite all the means she had at her disposal. She was grateful to have burst out of her bubble. She leaned closer to Chaim, touching his body with hers.

"Does she know about us?"

"I haven't seen her in a while, but I'll tell her next time."

They continued along the dirt track for a time, their fingers entwined, their arms swinging in sync. It felt like even their hearts were beating in harmony.

"No brothers or sisters I haven't heard of yet?" She looked up at him, taking in his perfect profile in the warm light of the setting sun.

"Nope. Only child."

"Me too."

They sat down under a carob tree and cuddled up in the last rays of sunshine.

"Is that what you'll study – law?" He picked a flowering straw of grass and started pulling it apart, seed by seed, sending her a few sideways glances.

"Yes. It's sort of inevitable, growing up with it being such a big part of our life. But I really love it too. The detail-orientation, the logical argumentation, the wide-reaching impacts. My parents always say it's nothing like on TV, but I don't mind the hard work."

"I know, my little toilet scrubber." His body gave hers a gentle nudge.

"Hey!" She slapped him playfully. He pulled her in for a kiss. They leaned back in the grass, enclosed by the earthy smell of the ground, still warm from another sunny day despite the evening dew setting in. Olivia looked up at the clouds drifting by.

"I just wanted to do something completely different first," she sighed and closed her eyes.

"Like falling in love with a kibbutznik?"

It was the first time either of them had used the word "love" in the presence of the other. A comforting warmth emanated from her core. She turned her head and looked deep into his soulful eyes. Chaim's wry smile revealed an edge of uncertainty which made her hesitate and reflect for a split second. Was their relationship just a temporary thing to him? And to her? She was so focused on living in the moment for once that she kept forgetting about the future. Or managed to repress it as much as she could when she was not daydreaming about the possible scenarios of a continued life with Chaim. She nudged closer into the nook of his arm and hugged him.

"Yes, like finding you, my love, and never letting go."

He kissed the top of her head and held her tight.

5

Twenty red roses, long-stemmed. The ultimate floral declaration of love. Exposing her promiscuity to the world. Everyone assumed they were from Chaim as their relationship had become increasingly public. Her own excitement quickly turned to shame when she read the small card. They were from Daniel. It was Olivia's nineteenth birthday and the extravagant flowers were delivered right in the lunchtime rush hour, inundating her with questions and comments from friends and strangers. Hannah and Lola knew. The rest she tried to brush off with awkward secret admirer jokes, before hiding the evidence of her deceit away in the kitchen. Vardit eyed her across the large pots she was scrubbing. Olivia looked away.

Chaim had invited her to celebrate with him at his place in the evening. He was lucky to have his own room – normally the teenagers had to share with someone until after the army. It was in a barrack like hers, only slightly bigger. He had a small woven rug on the floor which made the sound ricochet less off the beige tiles. He had proper lamps as opposed to her fluorescent strip lights, giving off a much cosier glow. And of course, he had the luxury of privacy.

She bounced up the small steps and knocked on his door.

"Welcome, birthday girl, to my humble restaurant," he greeted her with his winning smile and led her inside by the hand.

The room was lit by candles alone. She had not imagined him being such a romantic underneath that rough surface.

"You did all of this? For me?" Her eyes were wide open taking it all in. He had set the table in the middle of the room. Small pastry pockets with meat and vegetables were arranged on a large plate with a colourful salad in a bowl on the side and a bottle of white wine. Mellow pop was playing on the stereo.

"Well, I had Tomer help a bit…"

Olivia giggled at the thought of the two tough guys baking in the tiny kitchen and lighting the candles. She threw her arms around his neck and showered him with kisses.

"You haven't tasted my food yet!" he laughed.

"I'm sure it will be just perfect."

He seemed apprehensive when they sat down and dove into the meal. He was uneasy in his chair and fidgeted with the label of the wine bottle. It was unlike him to be nervous. Or was he annoyed with something? She could not tell. As usual he was hard to read. He had not been at the dining hall for lunch, but she was certain he must have heard it from someone by now. She looked at the small, vibrant bouquet in the middle of the table.

"They're not roses, I know."

She caught his eyes. The shame brewed inside her.

"Is it true? Do you have a boyfriend back home?"

Olivia averted her eyes and cleared her throat.

"Well, technically…"

"What do you mean 'technically'?"

"Just let me finish, please." She placed her hand on his. He let her leave it there, despite his agitated state. She took a deep breath.

"We did not actually break up, but in my mind I left him the moment I left home."

"Why did you not tell me this?"

"I tried to tell you, but…"

"But what?"

"There was never a right time…"

Chaim shook his head and pulled his hand away.

"Do you know how this makes me feel? Can you imagine what my friends are saying? And my parents?"

"I'm really sorry," she pleaded. Her cheeks were burning. She had not thought of his family at all. Her stomach churned at the thought of her deceit. It was completely out of character for her. It just felt so right to be with Chaim that anything and anyone else became insignificant.

"Not the greatest thing to be hearing from your mother."

"Your mother?" Olivia stared at him and stopped fiddling with her napkin.

"Yeah, Vardit was kind enough to tell her good friend the news of the day." His lip curled in a sarcastic smile.

Vardit? That conniving cow! Olivia's body tensed even further.

"This is a small community and this is my life."

She gulped. "I'm not trying to ruin your life."

"I know." Chaim ran a hand through his hair. "It's just… You'll be backpacking around soon, and I'm leaving in two weeks. I need to be able to trust you."

"What? Two weeks?" Olivia shot out of her slumping. Where was this coming from all of a sudden?

Chaim sighed and leaned back in his chair.

"I got the final details on my deployment yesterday. My start date is the same, but my location is now confirmed. I'm going to the Mitkan Adam base, near Jerusalem. It's Special Forces."

Chaim struggled to hide his pride at the last statement which was lost on Olivia in the moment. She was being pulled apart from the inside. Of course she had known he was leaving for the army soon – she had known it from the beginning. But Chaim had never mentioned a specific date; an actual final day made it so real and so close. She could not imagine life in the kibbutz without him. She could not imagine life without him, period. She could not even think about all the terrible things that could happen to him once he left the safe confines of their little bubble. The sound of Special Forces sent shivers down her spine. They looked at each other. Tears started streaming down her cheeks. A foreign sensation of stupidity came over her. Why was she acting like it was all a big surprise? She had lulled herself into an uncharacteristic state of denial on all accounts, blinded by her overwhelming feelings for him.

Chaim got up from his chair and kneeled down beside her. He held her face between his strong hands.

"Hey, I don't give a shit about that other guy if you don't. But you've got to be honest with me." He looked deep into her eyes. She nodded and sniffed then put her hands on his. He held her gaze in silence for the longest time, his lips moving slightly without a sound as if he needed a run-up to what he was planning to say next.

"*Ahuvati sheli, ani ohev otach.* I love you, Liv."

A thousand dragonflies soared inside her, lifting her heart and soul to the sky.

"I have wanted you ever since I saw you eat that mango. Now you are mine, I will not lose you."

The endorphins were pounding through her veins, rushing to her head. Her hands were shaking as she cradled his face.

"I love you too. *Ani ohev otach.*"

He chuckled. "It's *ani ohevet otcha* when a woman says it to a man."

She blushed. She had forgotten that pretty much all words were gender specific in Hebrew.

"But who cares! You love me! And man, do I love you!" He scooped her up, kissed her passionately and landed them both on the bed where they surrendered to each other's embraces. They had no time to lose.

Olivia broke up with Daniel the next day. Over the phone. She was ashamed to do it this way after all these years. He did not deserve this. But he did not deserve being kept in the dark either. Their relationship had run its course. There was no reason to drag out the pain any longer. Nevertheless, Daniel's incredulity, hurt and loath-ing seeped through the receiver and into her ear. Olivia convinced herself it was the right thing to do; the only thing to do. Yet her chest was still heavy after she hung up. Charlie's words suddenly reappeared at the back of her mind. Did she truly love Chaim? Or was she in love with the idea of being in love with him – aided by her hor-mones in overdrive in a foreign land? The moment she saw him coming up the stairs to the dining hall, greeting her with his dazzling smile, any doubt vanished. He was the most amazing guy she had ever met, perfect in every way; perfect for her.

Olivia browsed around the library, running her finger tips over the backs of the used books. The light was limited in the barracks, only two small windows along one side let-ting in the late afternoon sun. The smallest, most spartan library she had ever seen. Yet the satisfying smell of books was universal. She let out a small sigh.

She picked up a worn copy of George Orwell's *1984* and flicked through the yellowed pages.

"Do you know it?"

She was startled by the sound of a female voice. She looked up and saw a petite woman with short, dark brown hair and a distinct Roman nose. *Chaim's mother?*

"I've read *Animal Farm*, but not this one. Is it good?" She smiled at the woman. *Does she know who I am?*

"It makes you think. Definitely worth a read."

"I'll give it a try then."

"Good. Do you have a library card? I haven't seen you in here before." The woman walked behind a small counter.

"No, it's my first time here. Been enjoying the sun up until now, whenever I was not working."

"A good book for the cooler days then?" The woman's eyes were not unkind, but as guarded as Chaim's had been when she first met him.

"Exactly." Olivia smiled at her and folded her hands on the counter.

"What is your name, please?"

"Olivia. Olivia Margaux-Alexander. With a hyphen."

The woman's pen paused on the index card. Her eyes gave Olivia a discreet once-over. She wished she had gone back to shower first instead of heading here straight from work, suddenly aware of the lingering smell of kitchen, the stains on her clothes and the dirty sweat on her skin. Her mother would have seethed with shame if she had seen her now. She smoothed her hair and stood a little taller.

The woman filed the index card and handed Olivia the book.

"You can keep it till you finish it, but it has to be handed back in the exact same condition." She gave her a stern look.

"I will take good care of it." Olivia smiled and politely said her goodbye.

The Danish girls were busy packing their smaller backpacks in their room. Olivia sat on her bed reading out
loud from her guide book:

> *"The heart of Tel Aviv is one of the city's old-
> est areas, dating back to the final years of the
> Ottoman era. It is home to dozens of Bauhaus-
> inspired buildings, many of which have been
> restored. The area also contains many monu-
> ments and structures that are integral parts of
> Tel Aviv's history, including the old City Hall
> building, the cemetery where respected Israeli
> politicians and authors are buried, as well as
> some of the country's most famous synagogues –
> including Ohel Moed on Shadal Street and the
> Great Synagogue on Allenby Street at the corner
> of Ahad Ha'am."*

Olivia paused for a moment, briefly wallowing in her pride
at having nailed the pronunciation, before she continued.

> *"The heart is one of Tel Aviv's most dynamic and
> trendy areas. It has something to offer nearly ev-
> ery visitor – amateur historians, fashionistas,
> art and culture enthusiasts, club-goers and gour-
> mands alike.*
>
> *The tree-lined stretch of Rothschild Boulevard
> is the area's main artery, and is one of the city's
> most charming and popular places to stroll, go*

for a bike ride or simply relax at a coffee kiosk or on one of the many benches.

The surrounding streets are home to the Tel Aviv stock exchange, art galleries, investment banks, prominent law firms and some of the city's most stylish dining and nightlife spots. The area's diverse character drives the 24-hour atmosphere: No matter what time of day, there are almost always people on the street in the heart of the city."

Olivia moved her eyes from the pages to the two girls who met her with equally surprised looks. The description was a distinct contrast to their current surroundings and somehow gave a much more European image than the one they had of the city.

"I know!" Olivia responded, astounded. "Not quite what I'd expected either, but it sure sounds like a place I want to explore!"

"Hmm… Who's written that guide book?" Hannah queried.

"Probably Israel's Tourism Council or something," Olivia laughed, but she still found it hard to contain her excitement at going on a day trip organised by the kibbutz for the volunteers. It would be a nice little taster too for the backpacking venture she had in store with her Danish girlfriends once they finished their work experience. Despite her head-over-heels infatuation with Chaim and the ticking clock of his looming departure, she desperately needed a break from the rural confines and daily hum-drum of serving food, washing floors and cleaning toilets for strangers. The one-day weekend in particular made the adventures she had come here to experience seem il-lusive. Back home the promise Saturday held of a whole Sunday still to come was such a solace and the essence of the weekend. Here, only Saturday was holy which meant by the time they had just recovered from their hangovers from Friday night, it was time to resume the six-day work week. Not exactly the way of life she had hoped for. She thought back to the photos on the brochures and posters in the agency's office. When was she ever going to get a tan like that when she was cooped up most of the day with her head in the toilets? She vowed to never work weekends again once she returned home.

They arrived in the vibrant city of Tel Aviv on the decisive day of her ultimate rebellious act: getting a tattoo. The me-tropolis was noisy and seemed enormous coming straight from the kibbutz. The traffic, the people, the shops – the bus terminal alone was like a giant ant hill of steel and ex-haust. Finding the tattooist, which had been recommend-ed to Hannah, was a challenge in itself.

During the bus journey Olivia had argued with Vardit about the organisation of the outing. Her nemesis and Yael were their tour guides for the day. Olivia had proposed some suggestions to make their schedule more efficient and to include a few more places she wanted to see – all of which Vardit had brushed off with a sneer whilst Yael kept quiet. Olivia's irritation clouded the first part of the excursion, taking in the main sights as planned by Vardit before breaking into smaller groups exploring the city on their own.

Olivia, Hannah and Lola had made a pact to commemorate their joint experiences away from home with individual marks of self-expression. Olivia had taken a while to be convinced and deliberated even longer over the size and design of this irreversible addition to her body.

It was a tiny tree with delicate leaves, the size of her thumb nail on the small of her back, only for the few select to see. The tree of life. It was more a symbolic act, a rite of passage, than a visual display. Nevertheless, she had a lengthy discussion with the tattoo artist about the exact design. Because it symbolised the meaning of her name – as well as Chaim's – it had to reflect her personality, rather than be some stylistic logo. The process was painful. The tattooist was disturbingly high on something other than life; Rage Against the Machine were blaring *Killing in the Name* out of the speakers; and the fact that blood ensued freaked her out even more. In her naivety she had just thought some kind of special permanent felt tip pen would be used. To top off the whole experience, Lola fainted and hit the floor when it was her turn to go under the buzzing needle. *Quel drame!*

The end result was spectacular and worth it. Olivia thought of her little tattoo as an elaborate beauty spot; a subtle sign that would become an integral part of her and who she was; a new and improved Olivia; her love for Chaim carved into her forever.

Despite its limited size, she freaked out by the time the girls got back to the kibbutz.

"It's so permanent! It can never be redone!"

"Calm down, Liv. It's beautiful – and tiny." Lola stroked her shoulder and gave her an encouraging smile.

"What if I regret it one day? What if… What if I have to go to a gala at the queen's palace?" *Highly unlikely, but still a possibility*. What would people think? What would her parents say? She could vividly imagine her mother's reaction! "*Catin*" she would call her. Her mother was not too posh to call her own daughter a trollop.

"But they won't even be able to see it!" Hannah sighed. "Are you going to wear a backless dress to see the queen?"

Olivia realised how ridiculous she was being. Yet it was not till she saw Chaim that she calmed down. She revealed the dainty artwork to him slowly that night, taking care not to bother the sore skin covered in a thin layer of protective cream.

"I love it. It looks like an olive tree." She could hear the smile in his voice behind her. "You can't kill an olive tree, you know. They live on for thousands of years."

He gently kissed the small of her back around her tattoo then continued up her spine, nuzzled her neck, before turning her around to face him, their foreheads locked together.

"You and me forever, *ahuvati.*" Their lips met in the softest of kisses.

Olivia was running out of the community building. She had received a letter from her grandmother and was eager to get back to her room to read it. In her hurry she did not notice them chatting around the corner until it was too late. She physically bumped into Vardit and Chaim's mother. All three women exclaimed in surprise. Perplexed and embarrassed, Olivia apologised to them both, but Vardit continued to huff and puff and scold her in a mix of Hebrew and English. Chaim's mother said nothing, just displayed a reproachful look on her face which turned into faint recognition. Olivia wished the ground would open beneath her and swallow her up. Eventually she slipped away in a stream of apologies and sheepish smiles, leaving the women to bitch and moan about her behind her back. Her track record with mothers was not exactly flawless, but talk about being in the wrong place at the wrong time! *How bloody unfortunate!* She was so mortified by the whole incident that she did not even want to tell Chaim about it. She hid in her room and took comfort in her grandmother's heartfelt words and familiar handwriting, wishing she was by her side.

"Liv! It's for you," Naomi shouted from across the hall and pointed at the phone on the wall.

Olivia swallowed a mouthful of mixed salad and couscous and walked through the dining hall.

"I think it's your *imma*," Naomi whispered as she handed her the receiver. Olivia sighed and rolled her eyes. Naomi stifled a laugh as she left.

"Olivia?"

"Bonsoir, *Maman*." Olivia attempted a cheerful voice.

"What is wrong with you?"

"Erm, nothing's wrong with…"

"Daniel is the perfect guy. Perfect family. Perfect ambitions. You will never find anyone like him again."

Olivia was taken aback. *So she's heard the news…* She cleared her throat.

"*Maman*, you don't understand…"

"I understand perfectly well, thank you very much. You're off gallivanting God knows where, doing God knows what, and not giving any thought to your future or people here back home who absolutely adore you."

"By people you mean Daniel, I assume." She could really use a glass of water to wash down the remnants of her half-finished dinner with that dryness she was sensing.

Her mother let out an exasperated sigh.

"Olivia, when will you understand that I only want what is best for you?"

"And you think you know better than I what is best for me?" Olivia pinched the bridge of her nose and squeezed her eyes tight. "What if I don't want someone like Daniel anymore? He might be perfect to you, but how do you even know what and who is perfect for me?" She flung her free arm out.

"Oh, *ma chérie*. Because I know you. I'm your mother."

Olivia snorted. "Since when did that qualify you for anything in my life?"

"Olivia! I will not take that tone from you."

"Listen, *Maman*, I need to go now or I'll miss my chance of having dinner." She glanced at the dining room where everyone was scrambling out of their chairs to the dishwasher room and started to file past her down the stairs with curious looks.

"But, Olivia…"

"Goodbye, *Maman*." She hung up with a satisfied slam.

The kibbutz threw a party for the last batch of its young ones to leave for the army this year. It was a disco in one of the industrial-looking barns. More a techno rave, though, by the sound of the music as Olivia approached the gathering, her body burning hot against the cold air. *Firestarter* by The Prodigy pounded through her abdomen as she bottomed another can of beer and entered through the metal door. The volunteers had been warming up together at their barracks before joining the party. Olivia was semi-drunk and craving Chaim's touch. She struggled to adjust her vision in the darkness and blinking lights. She spotted him from the back on the other side of the hall.

She strode through the crowd across the dance floor and sneaked up behind him till her breasts touched his back. She put her arms around his waist and slid her hands into his front pockets, caressing his inner thighs through the thin lining whilst whispering in his ear:

"Oh, how I've missed you, mister!"

She caught the girl's eyes before his; the shock and disbelief painted on her face; the scorned lover of the young man whose private parts Olivia was one millisecond from fondling. She froze as he turned his head, his face completely unfamiliar and his voice far from the husky one she was expecting.

"Think you've got the wrong guy." The victim of her overt display of affection gave her a puzzled, but pleased look before the penny finally dropped. Olivia pulled her hands out of his pockets like they were on fire, mortified and apologetic, not knowing whether to laugh or cry, frantically looking around the room for her man whilst stuttering, "I'm sorry. So, so sorry."

She backed away from the stunned couple, stumbling over her feet, briefly wondering who they were. She caught Chaim's eyes, watching her from the make-shift bar flanked by Ben and Tomer. His mouth was wide open, but he had a twinkle in his incredulous eyes. *Thank goodness!* She rushed to his side.

"Come here, you silly *bahurah*! What am I going to do about you?" He stretched his arm out and pulled her in for a comforting squeeze. His arms remained firmly around her lower back as he scanned her face.

"Oh my… I don't know what to say. I am so sorry! I thought it was you! I really did!" Her heart was still throbbing and her cheeks burning. Her mind was suddenly sober, but her body was desperately trying to catch up. She struggled to get the words out right, the shame contributing to tying her tongue into a knot.

"I would damn well think you did! That kind of special treatment should be reserved for me only!" He broke into his irresistible laugh, and she surrendered to the relief of being in his arms and the alcohol flowing through her veins.

He kissed her – a firm, warm, wet kiss with his vigorous, playful tongue greeting hers, inviting it to dance as the music pounded from the speakers, claiming and cherishing her all in one move. He tasted of saltwater and chocolate, beer and honey. She wanted to devour him to the last drop. The floor was spinning and her body was tingling.

"Let's get out of here. I want you. Now." She cradled his face and looked deep into his eyes.

"Hmm… I think I can be convinced." Chaim arched one eyebrow and gave her butt a determined squeeze. He turned her back against his front and led her out into the cool night, his body firmly embracing hers, the two of them inseparable.

The inevitable moment came. The first day of Chaim's journey into the unknown. Olivia could not stop crying.

When would she see him again? How would she speak to him? How would her life in the kibbutz continue without hearing his voice and feeling his presence every day? So many questions, uncertainties and fears – all pitching in to create a dark void inside her.

It rained, of course – for the first time during her entire stay in Israel – like in some clichéd romantic film, as if even the skies above had to emphasise the inescapable misery of this day, forcing their passionate, yet still so brief relationship into uncharted territory.

"Remember, this is not goodbye, my love. I will see you on my first day off."

"But when will that be?" The return date on her ticket was looming in the not so distant future, scheduled for Christmas.

"I don't know yet, but I will call you."

She felt like a baby clinging to its parent, helpless and vulnerable. There was nothing they could do to prevent this. She had to let him go. He kissed her tears, one by one, before his lips met hers in a final kiss.

"Stay safe, *ahuvati*."

Her heart had left with him. She was numb inside. No more tears to cry. No more ecstatic joy to carry her through the day. She kept herself occupied planning her travels with the girls. Their time in the kibbutz was coming to an end, and they were organising their grand tour of the Middle East. The rain continued on and off for days, accompanying their preparations. Olivia tried to jump on the train of excited expectations on which Hannah and Lola were riding. Pippa and Bridget were going home soon. The guys were staying in the kibbutz for another few months. The Danish trio was off on new adventures. Yet her own future suddenly seemed uncertain.

6

The day before the girls set off on their tour of Egypt and Jordan, 62 people – mainly tourists – were shot dead at the Temple of Hatshepsut near Luxor. They got the news from Lola's parents who called their daughter on the verge of hysteria. Olivia decided to make a sense-check call to her stoic father. Either he was not worried or he hid it well.

"Just steer clear of the main tourist attractions for now. I'm sure the security levels are higher than ever for foreigners in Egypt at the moment. But just to be on the safe side," he reassured her.

Nevertheless, they did not want to be walking targets with their backpacks for all to see. So they changed their route to stay away from mainland Egypt: first stop the Jordanian embassy in Tel Aviv; then Amman, Aqaba and Petra; followed by Eilat en route to Dahab – a favourite backpacker hotspot in Sinai and a must-see according to their predecessors in the kibbutz who had passed on travel tips to the British lot. The grand finale was Jerusalem, where Olivia would reunite with her beloved soldier-in-training, before returning to work in the kibbutz for another few weeks.

They researched their maps and made notes of the border crossing points, as well as any visa applications they would have to incorporate into their travel plans.

Crossing borders in the Middle East turned out to be the most nerve-racking thing Olivia had ever experienced. It was the frustration and anxiety at having to empty your heaving backpack for the border police to rummage through in search of illegal items, such as women's magazines which were basically considered pornography in this region. It was having to explain in broken English why three girls were travelling on their own and what the purpose of their visit was.

Yet nothing in their travels so far compared to the fear that gripped Olivia when her passport was taken away from her by Arabic-speaking men, as she sat in a minibus crossing through no-man's-land between Israel and Jordan. It was the one thing she knew she could never lose. She was nobody without her passport. But they had no choice as the adamant border patrol unit insisted they hand their documents over. It was the longest hour of her life. Sitting on that bus packed with strangers, enveloped by darkness as it travelled through the desert, painstakingly slow and with several abrupt breaks for different search procedures to be completed. The panic was written across the faces of the three girls, their racing heartbeats audible, their distress palpable. Finally, they reached a small building where they were let out and ushered through the fluorescent-lit hall, their footsteps echoing across the tiles, for another X-ray screening and search of their belongings before they were handed their precious passports at the exit. Deflated and disoriented they now found themselves on the outskirts of Amman. They were immediately heckled by a group of taxi drivers. The girls saw no choice but to surrender to one, as they had no idea where they were nor where they were going.

They were dropped off in what had to be downtown – Olivia had tried to trace their route on her map in the dark taxi – outside a narrow building with a shabby façade displaying a chipped sign stating "OTEL". The "H" had broken off at some point. Or perhaps it had been an "M"? They checked in and made phone calls to their parents informing them of their whereabouts, just in case.

The room was surprisingly cool. It only had one window overlooking the roof of the adjacent building. Olivia pulled the curtains, but jumped at the sound of a bang on the window. The girls looked at each other. Another bang. Hannah was the one to take action. She peeked through the flimsy fabric and jerked when the pane was hit by an object. She recoiled and exclaimed:

"He's throwing stones at us!"

"Who?" Lola's voice was shrill.

"There's a man on the roof over there," Hannah pointed. "He must have seen us enter."

Olivia had never felt endangered by her gender like this before. How could they have been so stupid to embark on this journey without any male company? She pinched the bridge of her nose, trying to think.

"I need to stretch my legs." Hannah sighed.

"Me too." Lola joined in.

Olivia glared at them. Strange men were throwing rocks at their window, and they were going to venture outside in the dark?

"Shall we check out the local hood?"

"I really don't think that's a very good idea at this time of day."

"It's just for a quick walkabout. We've been cramped on buses all day."

Were they going to leave her here on her own? Olivia tried to weigh up the risks, but her mind and body were so tired.

"I'm staying in. You go without me. If you're not back in an hour, I'm calling the police."

Lola giggled and Hannah gave her an overbearing look, then closed the door behind them.

"Did you take a key?" Olivia shouted after them.

"Yes!" they shouted back from the stairway before they disappeared in sniggers.

Olivia locked the door and went to the bathroom. The smell was overpowering. A hole in the ground, a bucket of water and a small sink. No seat. No toilet paper. No shower. *Fantastic!*

This place was even more primitive than their kibbutz room. For the first time a small pang of homesickness hit her. A golden image of her spacious, cream-coloured bedroom in her parents' mansion flittered across her retina. *Well, you wanted foreign and exotic – you sure got it!*

It was what people least expected of her. She could have followed her girlfriends pursuing their glamorous dreams of studying French at the Sorbonne; or joined her numerous other peers backpacking through Australia; both fairly capital-intensive options. However, she was determined to get by completely on her own without any financial support from her parents and the expectations, as well as emotional strings, this implied. The time had come for her to just be her. Whatever that meant.

She found a pack of wet wipes in her backpack and cleaned her hands methodically, then brushed her teeth and rinsed with a swig of bottled water, only entering the bathroom to spit whilst holding her breath.

She knew Hannah and Lola occasionally found her too anxious and particular about certain things. Combined with her ingrained insistence on always being right, she often sensed she was alienating them. She only had a handful of close friends back home – probably for the same reasons. The three of them were indeed unlikely friends, but the circumstances had forged their friendship, and to be honest she could not imagine her recent and current adventures without them. None of her friends in Denmark would ever have found themselves in situations anywhere close to where and what she had been through over the past few months. She dropped down on the metal bed, kicked off her dusty shoes and dirty trousers and tried to get comfortable. She thought of Chaim. What was he doing right now? How was he feeling? She longed to caress his face. She pictured herself tracing her finger down his muscular back and his eyes lighting up with desire as she drifted off to sleep, physically and emotionally exhausted from an eventful day.

"We know it sounds crazy, but just hear us out."

Olivia frowned and shook her head at the girls. They had barged back into the room, bouncing like Duracell bunnies, startling her out of her doze.

"They are engineers…"

"Well, then it's all okay!"

"I would probably have reacted the same way as you if I had not met them. But they were really nice and polite and spoke English very well," Hannah continued.

"And they just happened to be going on a holiday to Petra and Aqaba at the same time as us?" Hannah and Lola's encounter in the *hookah* place around the corner sounded too good to be true. "What was in your *shisha*, ladies?"

"Listen, it's a free ride and we'll have male protection all the way."

"Or maybe we'll need protection from them!"

"What do we have to lose?"

"Erm, our lives? I don't know about you, but I personally have no plans of ending up raped and buried in a ditch in the desert!"

"If you would just meet them…" Lola pleaded.

"What, now? It's 11pm, we have travelled all day, and we've got a fully-packed day tomorrow exploring Amman."

"Okay. How about we all sleep on it, and then we'll make a decision tomorrow," Hannah reasoned.

"Fine." Olivia sighed. *Are they out of their minds?* Not a thousand Arabian horses would get her on board with this outrageous plan.

They were woken up by the sound of the call to prayer from the minarets. Olivia could tell that her fellow travellers were not as keen as her on her packed itinerary for their sightseeing. But she did not care. They had wanted to stretch their legs, right? And she wanted to make the most of her time in this country to which she was unlikely to ever return.

They took a taxi to the ancient ruins of Jerash outside Amman. The description in Olivia's guidebook did not do the place justice. It was the most impressive archaeological site Olivia had ever seen – even giving Rome a run for its money. It was so well preserved with a full-blown amphitheatre, a hippodrome, a forum, a temple and colonnaded, paved streets – an entire city giving a lifelike impression of how life in Greco-Roman times would have been. There were no other tourists in sight, just a few locals scattered around. Olivia found herself walking between columns and carved fountains, each sand-coloured stone oozing of history, with her imagination running wild and her mouth wide open in awe of the past present at this place. She snapped away with her camera, eager to store her memories, yet fully knowing that nothing she did could capture the splendour and authenticity of the atmosphere. She would have to do her best to store all her impressions in her mind forever.

The girls' sightseeing in Amman was rewarding, but challenging. Harassment, spitting, ogling, evil looks, pushing and groping... Travelling unaccompanied in this part of the Middle East was unheard of for young, Western women – and in retrospect unwise and culturally insensitive. But here they were, every moment left feeling like they had no rights or value. Olivia hid behind caps, sunglasses and boyish clothes, protecting herself from unwanted attention. Hannah was the most vocal objector of the three, shouting and swearing at any local aggressors, occasionally pushing back with her sturdy physique, making Olivia worried they would end up in a Jordanian prison. Lola was the least aware of her surroundings and often the cause of their maltreatment, showcasing her white limbs and light hair like a model on a treacherous runway. Olivia could not tell if it was down to genuine obliviousness or she did it out of spite. After several frustrated comments and reprimands from both Olivia and Hannah, it became clear that Lola did not care. She was going to be herself no matter where they went and who they met. Meanwhile, her travel companions prayed that they would survive her antics.

After two days they had all had enough oppression to last a lifetime. Luckily they were able to just leave. The indigenous women were not so fortunate. Although they were most likely carried in higher esteem than three Scandinavian girls roaming the streets alone.

It was a frustrating decision after all the efforts they had gone through to obtain a visa, followed by the hardships of entering the country, but they decided to cut their tour of the capital short and head south sooner than planned – falling in place nicely with their arisen transport opportunity.

Despite her livid objections, Olivia found herself sitting in a minivan with three foreign men, speeding through the desert with a racing mind and heart. The girls had all gone back to the hookah joint the following evening and introduced Olivia to their potential new travel companions. The place had turned out to be cosy and clean; and the Jordanian engineers were of course really nice guys – Abdel, Reza and Faisal. They had all studied in Paris, so Olivia in particular was able to make easy conversation with them in French. They were keen to practice their English and hear about Denmark too. They did not act inappropriately or make the girls feel unsafe in any way, but just seemed genuinely curious about their culture and background. Still, all Olivia's senses remained on high alert.

The protection of their new local acquaintances was a double-edged sword. Driving through the city and then the desert in a minivan kept the girls out of harm's way. Yet Olivia could not help thinking that she had left her brain in Denmark when boarding that plane into the unknown. The pleasant small talk bubbled between the guys and girls in delightful tones of broken English – all the while Olivia's mind reviewed emergency exits and escape plans. She felt trapped in the backseat of the van and her efforts to engage in the chat became half-hearted. Her body was tingling. The van was air-conditioned so it was not the heat that was bothering her. *Am I coming down with something?* A billion strange bugs could have made their way into her system during the past few days. She glanced at the others, gauging the mood and movements, observing the interaction, wary of any signs of danger. She caught Hannah's eyes. She seemed her usual stoic self.

The guys suddenly switched to Arabic and sounded agitated. Abdel turned from the front seat, gesturing to the girls.

"You have to climb in the back. Hide under the blankets."

Olivia's adrenaline levels exploded.

"It's the police. Up ahead. They will ask questions. It's better they don't see you." The voice of Faisal, the most fluent English-speaker of the three, was courteous, but adamant. There was going to be no discussion.

How was it better to hide from the police? Surely, they were there to protect people?

When he saw Olivia's questioning look, he ushered her, stating, "We'll all get into trouble!"

She reluctantly unfastened her seatbelt and got in the back of the driving van with Hannah and Lola. The three girls exchanged anxious looks as the vehicle slowed down. They lay in the semi-darkness. There were no windows, and their heads were covered. The synapses in Olivia's brain fired and connected, each thought produced more disturbing than the previous. The police pulled them over at a checkpoint.

"As-salaam alaikum!"

"*Wa alaikum assalaam.*"

The conversation was muffled. Olivia assumed the police were enquiring about their purpose and destination. Her heart was beating in her throat. The taste of metal in her dry mouth. What had they been thinking? How had she been persuaded into believing this road trip with three complete strangers, in a completely foreign country, would be a great idea? Should she continue to play along with their scheme? Or make herself known to the police? How desperate was she to travel to Petra and Aqaba? What would the consequences be of remaining in the back of the van? And the opposite? They needed to get back to Israel as soon as possible – this country was not for young girls to roam around at will, unaccompanied by fathers, brothers or husbands. They needed to get to the border – and cross it safely.

The police let them pass without further inspections. The girls could breathe freely again, more or less unscathed by the incident. Yet Olivia could not hold in her frustration any longer.

"I told you this was a terrible idea," she hissed in Danish as they scrambled back into their seats.

"They protected us, didn't they?" Hannah hissed in reply.

"What? They put us into a dangerous situation that could have developed into something unforgivable!"

"Well, it didn't. And none of us are hurt in any way." Hannah adjusted her clothes and looked down at her worn sports sandals.

"Girls, you're being rude to our hosts," Lola shushed. *Now she suddenly becomes aware of etiquette?* Olivia was fuming and stared out of the window for the remainder of the journey, her lips tight and her fingers tapping her crossed arms.

Arriving at the heart of Petra made Olivia's own heart race for whole other reasons. In that breath-taking moment, it was worth the entire nerve-racking drive. The sunlight danced on the red rock face as the Rose City unveiled itself to her in the middle of the barren desert. Walking through the secluded valley surrounded by rugged mountains, she could understand why this lost city had been hidden from the world for hundreds of years. The odd travel companions approached through the long narrow gorge, the Siq, in a state of peaceful veneration, their steps through the sand and the murmur of a handful of other tourists the only accompanying sound. The shade of the walls changed like a magical rainbow of ancient minerals from red over gold to cream by each step they took on the path leading up to the most famous element of this impressive cultural sight: the Treasury. It was in fact a royal tomb carved from sandstone in every colour from ochre to purple, immediately recognisable to Olivia as she had seen it in an *Indiana Jones* film. The wonders of the Nabataeans and their skills were awe-inspiring. She soaked up the history, its significance and splendour palpable, and struggled to fathom that this was all created by humans, yet within the phenomenal contours of nature. As she walked in the warm sun with her neck tilted back and her jaw dropped, she wondered about the looks and lives, motivations and struggles of these extraordinary, skilful nomads – now all gone and only these impressive stone structures remaining of a whole people.

Past the Treasury the hidden valley widened to reveal the remains of the city, including dozens of ancient tombs. By the time the quietly chatting, multilingual group reached the Monastery, an impressive monument scenically perched above the valley in the magnificent Petra Hills, Hannah and Lola were moaning.

"We have walked and walked for hours! I think we're done now," Lola groaned.

It put an immediate dampener on the beautiful views, but even Olivia's feet were beginning to feel the strain of their many steps through the dry dust which formed a fine layer on their skin. She was sticky from sweat. Devouring this splendid sight had made her lose track of time. The sun was setting and they had to hit the road soon to reach Aqaba in time to find a room for the night somewhere. They stocked up on drinks at a touristy café and made their way back to the minivan.

As she had feared, they arrived very late in the coastal town and most places were closed for the night. Nevertheless, their gallant companions managed to find a couple of rooms in a small, modest hotel. Olivia thanked them, and the girls settled down for a good night's rest after another eventful day; the door to their hotel room safely locked and double-checked by Olivia herself.

The next day the guys showed them around town, the highlight being a proud display of an allegedly very old boat. The girls struggled to contain their disappointment at the sight of a small wooden dinghy.

"It is 200 years old!" Abdel exclaimed with gleaming eyes and made a sweeping gesture towards the relic.

"We're Vikings. We've got thousand-year-old boats!" Hannah remarked drily.

Lola and Olivia smiled apologetically.

The historical sightseeing thus concluded, they went to the beach to kick back and enjoy the sun. Olivia was unable to relax and struggled to sustain the stilted conversation with their polite Jordanian acquaintances. She kept glancing sidelong at the only other woman present, covered from head to toe under a parasol whilst her husband paraded around in the world's tiniest speedos. As usual Lola was the only one who did not mind, and she lounged on the sand in her spaghetti-strapped top and shorts, drinking in the warm rays undeterred by any ogling onlookers. Olivia hid behind her sunglasses and her camera, snapping photos of the beautiful sea and the dark mountains on the horizon. *Well, at least you're not stuck inside polishing napkin dispensers and scrubbing floors anymore.* She hugged her trouser-clad legs, boiling under the Arabian sky. An awkward hour later, the girls thanked their helpful hosts and parted ways. Another border crossing was on the agenda.

7

Arriving in Eilat was like entering a different world. The beach was teeming with tourists. The women were uncovered. The night life was buzzy.

The girls found a hostel for the night. The landlady took payment upfront and gave them directions to the nearest places to buy food and stock up on basic supplies for their onward journey. They splashed out on a meal at McDonalds, celebrating their successful return to safe territory with burgers and French fries. They knew they would be back to living off flatbread and bananas soon enough, saving every shekel, dinar and pound they could. For now, the trio rejoiced in each other's company; free and alive.

Olivia bought postcards for her family and Amalie. She had not told her parents about Chaim, but she longed to share their love with the world. She thought about it for a while then put it into words on the card for Amalie. Seeing it written down, her scribbles in blue ink on white, made it real. *I have met someone. He is amazing. You'll love him.*

It was a statement to herself as much as to her friend. The pain of his absence in her daily life kept tightening its grip, making it harder to numb with each day passing in spite of all her adventures. Her fingers traced the words and a tingling spread through her body. She posted the cards with a hopeful heart.

That night Olivia took the opportunity to use the hostel's payphone to call her parents and Chaim. She desperately hoped he would be free to speak. An unknown male voice answered brusquely.

"*Halo?*"

"Oh, hello. May I speak to Chaim Rosen, please?"

"*Ma amart?*" The line was crackling.

"Sorry. *Ani lo medaberet ivrit.* Do you speak English?"

"Yes. Of course. Who is this?"

"My name is Olivia. I would like to speak to Chaim Rosen if possible, please." She found herself almost shouting now.

"Chaim Rosen? Sure." She heard the guy call out. It sounded muffled, as if he was covering the receiver with his hand. She imagined the surroundings. *A hallway maybe?* The sound of the stranger's voice had seemed to echo off the immediate walls and floor, rather than into a large canteen or the like. Chaim was panting when he got to the phone.

"Liv?"

"My love!"

"Are you okay?"

"Yes, I'm great. I just got back to Israel and wanted to hear your voice."

"I'm so happy to hear yours too." His breath calmed down. "How are you?"

"I'm okay. Keeping busy. How was Jordan?"

"It was interesting. Beautiful – saw some amazing sights. Not sure I'll ever be going back, but…" She trailed off and hoped to leave it at that.

"Hmm." She could hear him analysing her response. He sounded tired.

"How have your first weeks been?"

"Not too bad." He cleared his throat.

"Are you sure you're okay?"

"I'm fine. Really."

She wished she could look into his eyes, touch him, hold him tight.

"I miss you. I can't wait to see you. Do you know when you'll be able to meet me?"

"Yes, I got Saturday off in two weeks. We could meet in the city."

"That's fantastic!" Warmth radiated through her body at the thought of being with him again.

"It is. I miss you so much too." He lowered his voice, but she could hear him smiling. She suddenly remembered that he must be standing in an open space with hundreds of ears within reach around him.

They agreed where and when to meet in Jerusalem. She was relieved to find a pen someone had left by the payphone. She ripped a page out of the old phone book on the shelf below, then carefully wrote down the name and address of the café. She would hold on to the note as closely as her passport. They chatted for a bit about her travel route before Olivia ran out of coins, and Chaim had to get back to polishing his shoes and lining up his gear for the following day of duty.

A few guys were seated in the courtyard of the hostel with rows of beer cans on the wooden table in front of them. They had been getting rowdy whilst Olivia was on the phone. She struggled to place the accent. *Australian?*

Or South African, maybe? She always got the two mixed up. They were all huge with broad shoulders. Suddenly one of them got to his feet shouting. The guy across from him jumped up too and shouted back, then pulled something out of his shirt pocket. Olivia saw the blade glinting as it caught the sparse garden light. She sped through the shadows behind them, her heart thumping, desperate to get to safety. She met the landlady on her way in and briefly alerted her to the trouble. Olivia locked the door to the girls' room behind her and dropped down on her bunk bed, ignoring the quizzical looks on the faces of Hannah and Lola. Despite her wanderlust and enjoyment of all her cultural experiences, she had reached the conclusion that she hated hostels. *Another nail in the coffin!* Even behind the locked door, her heart was still pounding in her throat. A shiver ran through her.

"Ugh, I can't deal with any more danger around me right now. I'm all for exploring and having fun, but I need to just… breathe and, and… be! Do you think we could do that for a couple of days, please?"

"Nobody wants to be in danger, sweetie." Lola sat down next to Olivia and caressed her shoulder. Olivia stared at her, then at Hannah.

"Sure." Hannah shrugged and turned over on her other side, her broad back now facing Olivia. *So much for sisterhood.*

After a new tedious border crossing and a precarious taxi ride at breakneck speed with harrowing overtakings, they arrived in Dahab – a small former Bedouin fishing village on the southeast coast of the Sinai Peninsula, turned a mecca for young, Western, adventure-seeking backpackers. The construction of a few hotel resorts had commenced in the distance, but for now primitive hostels, guesthouses and provisional diving joints ruled this desert oasis. "Welcome to Dahab! It means gold in Arabic, you know. They say the gold washed down from the desert mountains to here where the town was built," the owner of their small hostel explained in beautiful English with a strong Arabic accent as he walked down the narrow corridor and showed them to their room. It was dark and humid. No windows to let in the sun or the air. *What, no sea view?* Olivia let out a snort at her wry, silent joke. Hannah gave her a strange look.

"The bathroom is down the hallway. Don't worry about the cockroaches. They don't bite. Enjoy your stay!" The owner smiled warmly and closed the door behind him. The girls looked at each other then jumped onto their beds as a couple of huge cockroaches darted across the cold, concrete floor.

Olivia read in her guidebook that the Bedouin meaning of the name Dahab came from the words "time goes". Allegedly, when you were here, you lost track of time as the days began to run together. It did not take long before she understood how the expression had originated. She had never before experienced such peace and quiet. Time stood still. The silence of the sand around them was as meditative as the gentle sound of the sea.

Olivia relished lounging on the beach, no longer on guard, the sun burning on her skin, finally getting her tan. Her bikini was tighter. Her food habits these past few months had been so different to her usual ones at home. First buffets every day of the week in the kibbutz, then white bread and deep fried food as they trod carefully with their culinary experiments, backpacking through these foreign lands on a tight budget. She must have put on a few kilos. Her first thought was what Chaim would say; then her mother's reaction appeared clearly in her mind. She shook it off and leaned back on her towel, closed her eyes and daydreamed of her impending reunion with her beloved boyfriend, a smile on her lips. The golden sand ran through her fingers like the hourglass of time.

The girls tried snorkelling for the first time, squealing as they spotted sea cucumbers, hyperventilating at the strange feeling of breathing through a tube. As she got used to the sensation of the equipment and the intense awareness of all the living creatures in the water, Olivia relaxed and marvelled at this whole new world opening before her eyes in the beautiful, vast blueness of the ocean and its colourful living beings.

They hitched a ride with a group of other backpackers on the rear of a pickup truck to go snorkelling at the Blue Hole – a place everyone they met mentioned as a must-see.

It was only Olivia's second time snorkelling, so she had her reservations. Yet nothing compared to the rush of adrenaline through her body when she ventured out over the steep drop into the infinite blue below her. She wished she could have shared all of these adventures with Chaim. The thought of his charming smile and soulful eyes made her dizzy with longing.

Only occasionally were they bothered: a couple of men covertly taking photos from afar of the girls in their bikinis; local Bedouin children running up to them to sell woven bracelets; and one particular waiter in a restaurant they went to a couple of times was very persistent in his approaches, especially towards Olivia, as the girls lounged on oriental rugs, smoking shisha and eating food from the fire pit. After a week he wanted to marry her and offered two camels to her father. Olivia politely declined many times, before she eventually got annoyed with his advances and had to avoid that part of the village entirely. She was tired of fending off unwelcome attention. Her yearning for Chaim and to be in his strong, caring embrace again amplified every day.

They were waiting for their laundry to finish at the small, clay-clad house of a local laundress. Hannah and Lola had wandered off to browse the simple stalls selling tourist souvenirs nearby. Olivia sat on a rock watching a Bedouin tend to his camels. The sun was setting, making the sky as golden as the sand. He caught her eyes and nodded with a modest smile. She reciprocated his greeting.

"Where you from?" he asked as he approached her, tilting his head to the side. His eyes were kind, his skin wrinkled from a lifetime under the ruthless sun.

"Denmark. Scandinavia." Olivia often found she had to explain the broader location of her small mother country in this part of the world.

"Ah. Cold there. Snow, yes?" His accent was strong, but he was keen to communicate.

"Yes, it gets cold in the winter." Olivia smiled.

"I never see snow."

Olivia lifted her eyebrows. Having grown up in the North, she could not imagine what it must feel like to live a life without ice and snow. She always longed for the warm sun.

"I never saw a desert till I came here."

The Bedouin gave her a wide smile then nodded pensively.

"You and me…" He gestured at them both. "Not so different."

Olivia looked at him quizzically, her hands resting firmly on her backpack by her legs as the old man took a step closer.

"We both wander. I am desert nomad. You are modern nomad." He pointed towards the vast desert behind them only a short distance from the village. "This. All of this my home. But I wander all my life. Look for grass and water for animals. I am not lost." His *keffiyeh*-clad head gave a small shake. His eyes twinkled. "I wander to be free."

Olivia's lips parted, but no words came out. She was still as the rock beneath her, processing the surprising revelation. She was a wandering soul and it was a gift, not a curse. A gift to continue to discover and explore for the rest of her life – not hide away, oppressed by the expectations of society, family and friends. Her whole body softened along with her mind. A bird in the sky caught her eye. It stood still for a moment, balancing on the thermals, frozen in time and space. The last rays of daylight gave the white bird a shade of orange as it dove and soared up into the desert sky.

Olivia broke into a beaming grin. She jumped to her feet and grabbed the Bedouin's hand, defying any cultural norms and practices of male-female interaction.

"Thank you! *Shukran!*" Her eyes sparkled as she shook his warm, weathered hand. A woman's voice called out behind her. Their laundry was ready. When she turned her head back, the Bedouin was gone and his camels too; but his words were etched into her soul. She stared with wonderment into the desert, feeling its warmth radiating through her. She bent down to put on her backpack and spotted a pebble by her foot. The fading sun reflected off its surface making it stand out in the golden sand. Olivia picked it up. It was smooth and bright white except for a black line running right through its centre. She turned it in her hand, puzzled over its significance. She brushed off the sand and slipped it into the pocket of her shorts with a smile.

After nearly a week of going with the flow, the girls decided to venture further afield to Mount Sinai – the place where Moses received the Ten Commandments according to Jewish, Christian and Islamic tradition. The girls' interest in the site was not for religious reasons, although for Olivia the historic value of the place could not be denied. Backpacker rumours had it that the sunrise from the summit was like none you had ever seen. The only way to experience this was to hike up the mountain in the dark. The owner of their hostel knew a driver who regularly took tourists out there. Soon Olivia, Hannah and Lola found themselves in a small group of other Westerners in a minivan driving through the desert at dusk. The terrain got hillier as they approached their destination. They were dropped off in the middle of nowhere surrounded by darkness, only to discover that none of them had brought a torch. Olivia kicked herself for being so unprepared. What had happened to her usual organised self? Dissolved in the desert sand?

They fumbled and stumbled along in the nightfall, only guided by a few other hikers up front who had the extreme wherewithal of donning head torches. Once again Olivia wondered what she had got herself into, driven by her quest for adventure, so far away from home.

She suddenly sensed the presence of a large, warm body right next to her. Two big eyes glinted in the dark. Olivia's brain was desperately processing the faintly recognisable smell when the beast let out a loud, offended huff. Her heart jumped – and so did her body to get out of the way from the grumpy camel resting on the side of the track. The girls increased their speed to keep warm in the cold night. They stopped at a hut where a Bedouin conveniently sold water, tea and the use of blankets for a small fee. They put on any extra layers they had brought in their small backpacks and continued their expedition. When they reached the flat plateau of the summit a few hours later, they were sweating from the hike, but they soon started shivering from the cold. It was impossible to keep warm when they were not moving due to the clamminess under all their layers, none of them breathable. Instead Olivia's thin, yellow raincoat intensified the dampness of her body. The girls pushed aside any social norms of personal space and huddled up with strangers for body warmth like lost sheep in an open field as they lay down on the dusty ground for a rest, waiting for the sun to appear.

It was indeed the most spectacular sunrise she had ever seen; an orange ball of fire above the black rugged rocks, spreading its golden light and warmth across the barren, alien landscape far below and onto the amazed faces of the gathered hikers. The outlandish efforts and experiences of the night had been worth it. Olivia closed her eyes and let the warm rays penetrate her soul. A moment of utter calmness washed over her.

It was a long walk back down – this time via the seemingly never-ending steps to Saint Catherine's Monastery at the foot of the mountain. *The 3,750 steps of penitence,* Olivia remembered from her guidebook. Her thighs and calves hurt by the time they got down. The temperature had risen again with the sun. The peaceful oasis of the old walls provided welcome shade as the girls sat down on a bench for a brief rest.

The basilica was open for visitors and Olivia ventured inside, leaving Hannah and Lola on the bench. She had never been in a Greek Orthodox church before. The relative darkness blinded her in contrast to the bright sunlight outside. The fragrant scent of incense was the first thing she noticed before her eyes acclimatised. She took in the rows of dark wooden pews, the intricate lanterns hanging from the ceiling, the ornate paintings and golden icons adorning the walls. She had read that it was one of the oldest working monasteries in the world, and she was impressed by the beautiful condition of the church. To her surprise she was the only one in there. She relished the peace and quiet and wandered around in silence, admiring the detailed mosaics of the floors and the richly decorated panels of the iconostasis – a complete wall of golden images depicting religious figures and scenes. To think such rich artworks and precious reliquaries – some dating back to the fifth century – were housed out here in the middle of the desert was mind-blowing to her. Olivia's reveries were startled by one of the priests entering the chapel in his flowing garments, covered from head to toe, only his vast white beard surrounding his face breaking up the blackness. She felt like an intruder, disturbing the balance of peace in this sanctuary. He gave her an indefinable look. She quickly averted her eyes and turned to leave. She put some coins in the collection box by the entrance, to contribute to the upkeep of this magnificent cultural heritage. Her mind and body were ready for respite after the intense stimulation of the last twelve hours.

Back in Dahab, the girls enjoyed washing off the sweat and dust at the hostel before venturing out for a much needed meal. They opted for plain Margherita pizzas in one of the restaurants catering for young tourists. Olivia briefly worried about the cheese, but it looked cooked through and she bit into the meal. The clientele was a prime target for street vendors and tour guides alike passing by the terrace of diners. The girls struggled to eat in peace. They were gritting their teeth by the time he approached them – professional and slightly less pushy than their previous suitors. He introduced himself as Hakim as he handed them his brochure and card. He offered them a unique experience – just the four of them and the Bedouins leading the camels into the desert. Olivia's fight-or-flight reflex kicked in. She watched Hannah and Lola listening intently to his sales speech, flicking through the colourful, flimsy pamphlet. The three of them were keen to explore the desert close up and not just from afar behind a window pane – but not at any price. Olivia questioned the zealous salesman about cost, payment, logistical provisions, duration, route and destination – anything she could think of whilst trying to analyse the guy and his intentions. His legs were short, his hair was oily, and his words were very persuasive. Hannah and Lola looked at Olivia, their eyes wide with eagerness. She bit the inside of her cheek and kept silent for a moment before she agreed with a brusque exhale.

"Camel safari under the stars it is then." Hakim rubbed his hands together, displaying a cocky smile. Olivia's heart sank.

She had never in her life seen so many stars. Foreign constellations and well-known ones, albeit the latter upside down. Even the crescent of the moon was playing tricks on her, lying down on its back like on a golden spire straight out of Arabian Nights. It was not just a quirky detail featuring in her childhood storybooks. This was truly what the moon looked like down here in the desert. Shooting stars were suddenly ten a penny as opposed to the astronomical unicorns of fairy tales.

Two Bedouins – father and son – led their camels into the dark desert where they camped half an hour's ride outside the village. The meal was primitive, but full of taste and scent, cooked over the small, open fire and eaten with their bare fingers. Olivia breathed in the calming, subtle smoke, as the light from the flames danced upon their faces.

Hakim had homed in on the girls like a predator, first targeting them with his tempting tourist guide talk back in the village, persuading them to let him accompany them into the desert and stay the night. Settled in by the small campfire he now approached them one by one, assessing his prey. As the small talk about cultural differences developed into a discussion of the perceived stereotypical frivolity of Scandinavian women, Olivia's jaw ached from clenching her teeth harder and harder. Was this his way of picking up girls? With ill-concealed offences wrapped in an ingratiating voice and obvious body language? Had this really worked for him before? For all her fellow female travellers out there, she hoped not.

With his smooth, but obnoxious operating, Hakim conquered Olivia's objections to letting him read her palm, like an innocent party trick, moving ever closer till she could feel his breath on her face. She watched his Adam's apple bobbing and was filled with disgust. Line by line he traced and babbled on, generic statements and ridiculous predictions. Then he uttered the explosive words: "Your mother".

Afterwards, she only remembered the shouting. The uncontrolled pitch of her voice bouncing off the nothingness of the empty desert. She had not meant to raise her voice, but she had been unable to control herself, triggered by the offensive insinuations of this random little man who had got so inappropriately close to her.

She recalled the shock on his face as he crouched under her unexpected rage, her shadow towering over him, and the silence of her travel companions as they watched her unravel in the cool sand, the only other witnesses the

Bedouin feeding the camels in the darkness behind her and his young son tending to the campfire. Everyone froze as she detonated.

She had grown up in a bilingual family with friends and class mates from all nations and religions, mainly children of diplomats and foreign executives. She believed she had a natural respect for others no matter their origins and faith – a positive advantage in an increasingly globalised world and when travelling and meeting new people. She knew Islam could be a beautiful religion and its roots were identical to those of Christianity and Judaism. But this condescending, despicable buffoon was making a mockery of it. And she was not even religious! To use religion to whack people – women in particular – on the head with patriarchal, archaic, misogynistic bullshit made her blood boil. To make it personal sent her over the edge.

Perhaps if she had not felt so oppressed already from their negative experiences travelling in the region. Perhaps if he had stuck to ranting off his absurd, hypocritical arguments of how modest virgins made better wives, how every man had the right to sow his wild oats with promiscuous Scandinavian blondes, and how the path to heaven – where more virgins miraculously awaited – went through the arches of his mother's legs. Perhaps then she would have kept her calm and confronted him with reason.

The physical violation of such proximity by a complete stranger was intimidating. Yet the fact that he thought he had the right to attempt to enter her mind through the lines of her hands, expose her, label her, make judgements on her family, and even question her strained relationship with her mother was worse. Should she have been afraid? Most likely. So many things could have happened in such a remote setting to which this dark stranger had managed to lure the three girls. Fear never entered her mind, though. She had been too angry and too shaken. Things might have turned out very differently. But they did not. Once more she was saved by fate, cosmic powers or her own survival instincts. She had exploded in a mad mushroom cloud of fury:

"What gives you the right to accuse me and my entire national gender of being mere slutty warm ups to your so-called sacred marriage? Do you think you can just read a girl's palm and that's your ticket to free sex in the desert? I have not read the Quran, but I am pretty sure that nowhere in your holy book does it give you the right to violate any female! I am an intelligent, open-minded young woman. I believe in freedom for all – religious, romantic and freedom of speech. But you have no right to judge me or my family. You do not know me. I do not owe you anything. You stay away from me and my friends! Or take us back to the town safely right now!"

The desert fell silent. All three girls held their breath. The Bedouin rustled the fire with a stick. Hakim recoiled, then struggled to replace the shock on his face with his sly smile.

"Calm down. I just read palm."

"What? You did not just…"

Hannah stepped in between the two of them.

"All right! That's enough. I think we all heard and saw what happened. You!" She pointed at Hakim. "You move over there and sit with your friends. We'll stay on this side of the fire. We'll all try to get some sleep and everything will look brighter in the morning."

It was impossible for Olivia to sleep. The adrenaline was pulsing through her body, and her throat was so tight she struggled to breathe. She did not know whether it was the guide or herself that shocked her the most. She was sick and tired of being in a constant fight-or-flight mode. She genuinely longed to be home. Home with her parents in their cosy little corner of this scary big world, in the safe centre of her universe.

They survived the nocturnal conflict in the desert and rode back on their camels in awkward silence. Olivia held her chin high in the morning sun. She refused any interaction with Hakim, but gave the Bedouin and his son as generous a tip as she could spare.

"So, do you want to talk about it?"

A tiny cloud of haze glided over the sun. The girls were sizzling on the beach, spread out like starfish on their towels.

"Talk about what?" Olivia adjusted her sun glasses. Her sweat made them slide down her nose whenever she moved despite lying flat on her back.

"Last night. In the desert." Lola stared at her, resting on her elbows. Hannah looked like she had dozed off next to her.

"What about it?" Olivia glanced at Lola sideways.

"The whole going ballistic thing. About your mother."

Olivia pondered. Did she want to share her issues with Lola and Hannah? They had shared so many other intimate things over the past few months. But were they *friends* friends? Would they remain friends long after their desert adventures were over? Could she really trust them? What would she gain from exposing her innermost secrets?

"I don't have a great relationship with my mum either. Her drinking and all that..." Lola trailed off.

Lola had only mentioned her alcoholic mother once before when they had all been drinking back in the kibbutz. Olivia appreciated her friend's attempt at trying to relate through her confession and to support her, but she did not need a shoulder to cry on. She needed the exact opposite. To *not* live in the shadow of her dominating mother. To live her own life. Olivia exhaled and turned onto her side.

"I'm sorry about that. Has she always been drinking?"

"As long as I can remember. Always hoping she would quit. And she did sometimes..." Lola gazed out at the Red Sea.

Olivia swallowed. Perhaps her mother issues were not so terrible after all. *Everything is relative.*

The girls spent another few days in tranquil Dahab, soaking up the sun – knowing they would soon enough be back in the depth of the Danish winter. Then it was time to make their way to the border crossing point of Taba to return to Israel. They had got used to the routine by now. The waiting in line and emptying their bags. The questioning and occasional body frisking. But this time was different. The border control guards were more aggressive. Every step took longer. Olivia wondered if they were on the lookout for someone or something specific, like a wanted person or drug smugglers. The girls were watched more intensely. They were pulled aside brusquely and asked to empty their backpacks. Olivia felt harassed again for being a woman, unfairly under suspicion – most likely in order for the police men to make the most of the welcome situation of having three young Western women all to themselves.

Suddenly, they were let into a side room. Olivia's heart pounded. Why could border crossing never be simple? She became nauseous from the stifling heat in the small room and the smell of sweat radiating from the guards; big wet patches under their arms, darkening their pale uniforms. She thought of her own soldier, a true gentleman; a far cry from these specimens in front of her – and diametrically opposed to the polite Jordanians who had accompanied the girls only weeks ago on the other side of the Gulf of Aqaba.

"We have rights. We are citizens of Denmark. We... We demand to speak to someone from the embassy." Olivia's stomach churned. Her voice sounded like a faint parody of herself. She could feel her hand tremble as she smoothed her hair. She clenched her teeth and steadied herself.

The older guard seated at the desk laughed in her face, seemingly surprised at her outburst.

"Rights? You are on Egyptian soil. You must follow Egyptian laws. You cannot do same here as home," he scoffed in broken English.

Why were they being held back? Was this a common occurrence? Were the guards trying to get money out of them? Or was it just a sick alpha male display of control, with this vile man getting a kick out of intimidating young girls? Olivia's throat was so tight she could hardly speak.

"Which laws exactly are we breaking? We have a right to be told. And to a phone call." She desperately searched her brain for a way out. Who should she call if she were granted a phone call? Her father or the local embassy? She remembered it was located in Cairo which was hours away from Taba. She glanced out the window. Israel was so close she could almost touch it. She thought of Chaim and nearly broke. She looked at the other two girls. Lola had not stopped crying since they were seated in the room. Hannah was pale and uncharacteristically silent. Olivia decided to change her tactics. No more victim playing. No more watching this pathetic excuse of a grown man flexing his power muscles. She could not spend one more second in this suffocating excuse for an office – let alone in a potential Egyptian prison!

She swallowed and leant forward, placing her underarms on the desk. It was sticky from the heat and grime.

She gathered her strength to control her voice. Calmly and with piercing succinctness like the venomous hiss of a snake her words rolled out one by one into the stale air.

"My father is a well-known international lawyer – Professor Arthur Alexander. I bet when the press hears you have held three Danish girls captive illegally, your government will be in a bit of trouble. Whatever tourists you have left after the shootings at Luxor will run away screaming and take their money with them. I would not want to be in your shoes when that happens. Imagine being responsible for an international diplomatic crisis – and for your country losing its number one source of income. Mubarak will have your head on a stick." She stared at him with defiance. Her gut might be a writhing mess, but her mind was now hard as steel.

The guard's face was expressionless, but she could tell by the look in his eyes that her tirade had triggered an avalanche of thoughts in his head. She hoped name-dropping the president alongside her father would have the intended effect. A nerve twitched by the side of his right eye. They held each other's gaze as the consequences of the possible actions and outcomes filled the dense space, the only sound accompanying their standoff coming from the futile fan whirring in a corner. The guard blinked then pushed back his chair, startling all three girls as the loud, screeching noise broke the silence. He got up and marched across the room to his colleague by the door. He spoke briskly in Arabic, spit spraying from his mouth. The younger guard caught Olivia's eyes then stared back into the empty space behind his superior. He answered him. The agitated older guard turned his head briefly, glancing at the girls, then left the room, slamming the door behind him. Hannah looked at Olivia, her eyes wide open. Olivia's heart was in her throat and she struggled to swallow, let alone respond to Hannah's questioning look. *Shit.* What if she had just got them into even deeper trouble?

"*Yalla!*" The girls jumped at the guard's shout. "Out!"

They exchanged scared looks.

"Where are we going?" Hannah had finally found her voice again.

"You go. Get your things. You go to Israel."

Olivia tossed her head back, her eyes to the ceiling, wiping the sweat off her upper lip with both hands as she let out the loudest exhale. They were free to go.

The Egyptian guards confiscated a few of their effects – an embellished knife Olivia had bought as a present for her dad, and a small shisha pipe with sweet tobacco Lola had picked up at a souvenir shop. None of the objects were illegal; Olivia had made sure. These guards appeared to have a different interpretation of the law. The act was more likely a desperate symbol of force – a consolation prize for their lost battle in the back office.

However, the girls did not care. They were pale and shaking as they gathered their belongings in silence. They walked out of the border control hall with determined, yet unhurried steps like sleepwalkers heading for an invisible reality.

They reached a bus stop before they all collapsed. Their backpacks fell heavy in the dust as the trio pulled each other in for a tight hug. Lola's body shuddered from intense crying. Even Hannah had tears in her eyes.

"I can't believe you did that." She squeezed Olivia's shoulder and stared at her with softness.

"You would both have done the same." Olivia shrugged with a smile and wiped her cheeks with her sleeve.

"No, I could never… You saved us," Lola sobbed and caressed Olivia's hair.

A bus pulled up, startling them out of their emotional moment, forcing them back into the surrounding world of decisions and practicalities.

The girls were relieved beyond belief to be back in Israel. It felt like home. They had had some amazing cultural experiences travelling through Jordan and Egypt, but despite the best efforts of their Jordanian acquaintances Olivia had never felt safe. In Israel any potential dangers were abstract, obscure and mainly out of sight. Here they could walk the streets unscathed. They could go to the beach in peace – even sporting bikinis they would only receive appreciative or flirtatious looks from fellow tourists. They could truly relax and enjoy the sun. Their sex was no longer a flashing neon sign stigmatising them, inviting harassment or instigating grounds for loss of freedom. They explored the marine life in Eilat and floated in the Dead Sea, taking photos of each other bobbing around like corks. Then they made their way to the Holy City: Jerusalem.

8

J erusalem. So much history in one place it was overwhelming. The cradle of three major religions; the
source and venue of so much hatred and fighting.
Three different cultures and people living side by side, all
originating from the same place. No guide books could
have prepared her for this. She struggled to explain the
emotions stirring in her. She was in awe.

They entered the Old City through the Damascus Gate
by chance, unknowingly walking straight into the Muslim
quarter wearing only vests and shorts, arriving straight
from the warm sun of the south. It was another phenomenal cultural faux pas despite their weeks of travelling in
the Arab world. They were pushed, shoved, shouted at and
hit with sticks by old women – until a merciful market stall
owner ushered them into his shop and showed them how
to cover up with demure scarves.

"*Shukran*," Olivia nodded at their saviour. Hannah and
Lola followed her lead.

He shook his head gently at the girls, but reciprocated
with a smile before he sent them back into the buzzy ba-
zaar full of colours, scents and sounds.

They located the small hostel they had found in Olivia's
guide book, unloaded their backpacks and made their
way to the magnificent Dome of the Rock. Its gold-plated
dome towered and twinkled on top of the Temple Mount;
its bright blue and green mosaic-clad walls beckoned you
to marvel at its wonder. Olivia had never seen so many different people's shoes before, all lined up side by side on

the white steps. The girls parked their dusty trainers too before entering through the entrance dedicated to non-Muslims. The peacefulness hit her like a wall of silence. It was surprisingly cool inside, and the heavy carpets under her feet softened her steps, the only sound coming from muted prayers whispered by the kneeling and rising worshippers. It was as splendid on the inside as it was on the outside. The walls covered in golden mosaics and Koranic verses. The marble pillars stretched up tall, carrying the weight of this impressive piece of architecture. The light from the arched windows high above, just below the circle of the dome, streaming down and catching the girls as they absorbed the impressions in veneration.

Olivia squinted against the bright sun as they exited and walked past the Al-Aqsa Mosque, the third holiest site in Islam. She stopped to take photos, desperately trying to capture this extraordinary place. She struggled to process the intensity of it all. Had Muhammad, Abraham and Jesus truly all prayed here at some point in time? Was it just the enormous presence of history that overwhelmed her? Or was there a touch of divinity in the air engulfing her in its magical embrace?

The Western Wall. The Wailing Wall. *Kotel*. A rose of many names. When they had passed the stern soldiers at the security checkpoint, Olivia was surprised by reaching a much more confined space than she remembered from photos. Despite its limited scope, the tall, sand-coloured wall still took her breath away. Black and white clad orthodox Jews, tourists and locals, praying and placing secret wishes on white pieces of paper in the cracks of the wall. Olivia walked up as close as she could, placed her hand on the ancient stones and closed her eyes to absorb its significance. She looked up and saw sprouts of green above her, growing from this renowned piece of history. A pigeon spread its wings and flew from its hidden nest, startling her – yet she could not help but smile. She knew this place would stay with her forever.

The following day they ventured outside the walls of the Old City and into Mea She'arim – one of the oldest Jewish neighbourhoods; this time carefully dressed in long trousers and sleeves, surrounded by black-clad men with large-brimmed hats, beards and *payot* – the long curly sidelocks – and women in long skirts and demure blouses. Olivia felt like she had stepped back in time and was slightly uncomfortable at feeling so out of place again. Yet at the same time she found the encounter fascinating, and the contrast of this ultra-religious and conservative community to the surrounding modernity was an eye-opening experience.

Olivia took pride in her map reading skills. Yet they still got lost in their quest to find the Knesset. She refused to give up despite the moaning and groaning from her travel companions and her own aching feet. At least they had changed out of their moderate clothes after leaving Mea She'arim and the temperature had risen. It was unusually warm for December, they had been told at the hostel. Jerusalem's elevated position normally meant day temperatures around 14 degrees Celsius. Olivia wiped her forehead with a pocket tissue and took a swig from her water bottle. The hilly roads meandered through a residential neighbourhood before they finally entered Givat Ram, the governmental campus where many of Israel's most important national institutions were located. She was victorious once they arrived, more pleased with her own success than the actual sight of the columned concrete, modernist mastodon towering above them. They had made it to another of her must-see places of interest. Once more she had persevered in her quest to explore as much of the world as possible.

The girls decided to opt for a taxi for their return journey to the hostel – mainly because Lola spotted it driving towards them whilst Olivia was packing away her camera. Hannah and Lola jumped in the back, leaving Olivia to the front passenger seat. The driver spoke little English but was keen to make conversation. It was not the only thing he was keen on, Olivia noticed as he kept leering at her bare legs. She cursed herself for having changed into shorts. It really was not that warm outside. Eventually he snuck his hand over and placed it on her thigh. Olivia froze. He was driving at high speed, and she was worried what would happen if she pushed him away.

"Girls, he's groping me," Olivia spoke in Danish as calmly as she could. "I really want to get out."

Hannah and Lola shifted in their seats to try to catch a look.

"You'll be fine – we're probably there soon." Hannah was rubbing her calves, and Lola could barely keep her eyes open.

"Erm, I'm not taking one for the team by letting a creepy stranger feel me up! Again!" Her mind flashed back to her desert meltdown. She was shocked at her friends' re-action. After all this time and all they had been through together? *Freaking lazy, selfish cows!* She was exploding now with anger at all three of them.

"We want to get off now, please." Olivia gestured at the driver who did not appear to understand, but just kept on sporting his sleazy grin. "Stop the car now!" Olivia shoved his hand away and grabbed the door handle.

"But cannot stop here. Big road!" He shrugged indifferently.

"Seriously, Liv, we can't just get out in the middle of the…" Lola was suddenly wide awake.

"I don't give a shit. I would rather walk in the middle of traffic than stay a second longer in this car! Stop now!"

The taxi driver started raising his voice and spoke Hebrew in a harsh tone – most likely cursing. Olivia could not understand the words, but she could tell from his body language that he was far from happy. She grabbed some money out of her neck purse and threw it on her seat after letting herself out onto the side of the road to the sound of honking and blaring vehicles. It was indeed full of heavy traffic and not a place for pedestrians, let alone three lost female tourists. It seemed to be the circular road running along the walls to the Old City. Olivia stomped on, fuelled by her anger and indignation, leaving Hannah and Lola panting along after her, dodging the speeding lorries and beeping cars. She did not stop till they had made it safely in past the walls.

"What the hell, Liv?" Hannah huffed when she caught up with her.

"You tell me, Hannah – what the hell?" Olivia fumed. "Were you going to let that creep sexually harass me for the whole ride to save yourselves from more walking?!"

"It wasn't like that…" Lola attempted.

"Really? Because to me it sure looked like that was exactly what happened back there!" Olivia's eyes pierced both girls, her nostrils flared, and she struggled to hold back her angry tears. "I thought we had each other's backs."

"We do… Sorry, Liv." Lola gave her arm a squeeze and tried to pull her in for a hug, but Olivia was too upset by the whole thing and could not help but step away. *Always the outsider…*

"I'm really tired – and you clearly are too." Olivia gave an ironic smirk. Lola averted her eyes.

Hannah sighed, shifting from one foot to the other. "Yeah, it's been a long day – let's get back to the hostel and get some rest."

They rose early the following morning. Olivia's feet were sore and her mind overflowing with impressions, yet her body tingled with excitement. Today was the day. The atmosphere was gloomy after the girls' fall out, and they ate their spartan breakfast of white toast, butter and jam with few words exchanged. It was Saturday – the Shabbat. The quietness of the empty, cobbled alleys of the Jewish quarter was almost deafening. It suited Olivia's mood well. They did not speak much as they explored, slowly making their way to the Christian quarter, each young woman walking in her own thoughts.

The noise levels increased as they approached their sights of the day along with a beehive of other tourists. As the Church of the Holy Sepulchre appeared before her with its imposing limestone walls and grey domes topped with golden crosses, Olivia could sense the buzz and veneration of the expectant crowd. Waiting in the long line to enter turned out to be worth the effort. The fact that she had entered the rock-cut tomb of Jesus and stood on the spot of his crucifixion convinced her that this historical figure must have existed – regardless of whether he was the son of God or this God was real. She traced the crusader graffiti on the broken marble columns fronting the basilica and smiled. The presence of so much history, such key artefacts and locations was just impossible to capture by either camera or words. Olivia was mentally and physically saturated after nearly three days of taking in this awe-inspiring city.

They followed the steep, winding lanes of Via Dolorosa, crammed with street vendors shouting and pilgrims carrying wooden crosses, retracing the steps taken by the cross-bearing Jesus on his way to crucifixion according to biblical history. Religious believer or not, this was a fascinating glimpse into the past. Olivia eagerly studied every panel and sign on the route to absorb as much information she could, putting all her impressions into the historical and cultural perspective they deserved. Hannah was losing patience with her, she could tell. Lola killed time by browsing through the offerings of the street vendors. Eventually they stopped for an early lunch.

"Are you excited about this afternoon?" Lola wiped some tahini from the corner of her mouth and smiled at Olivia. Olivia swallowed her falafel and returned her smile.

"I am. Very much."

Her pulse quickened at the thought of seeing Chaim again. It was the ultimate culmination of an eventful month of travelling – the long-awaited and highly desired cherry on top. The image of him was vivid in her mind, but she longed to feel his touch after so long apart. She hoped the coordination of their rendezvous over the phone would be successful. She was suddenly desperate to return to the hostel to get herself ready.

She did not recognise him till he stood right in front of her. It was the first time she had seen him in uniform. His arms flexed under the khaki shirt as he stretched them out to greet her. His tanned face broke into a huge grin and his eyes sparkled. Her jaw dropped. Her heart raced. *Holy shit, this guy is my boyfriend?* She leaped into his arms and met his lips in a passionate kiss. He hugged her tightly, lifted her off the floor and swung her gently from side to side. They both burst into laughter.

"Man, how I missed you!" His husky voice was rich with emotion.

Olivia could hardly speak, her relief overwhelming, her heart overflowing. She was just one big ecstatic smile. They managed to compose themselves enough to order drinks and some snacks at the counter before settling down at one of the metal café tables inside.

"You look so good in your uniform! I'm so proud of you." She reached over to caress his wrist, her voice bubbly when she finally regained it. She felt informal and inadequate in her washed-out dress, despite having gone through considerable efforts choosing the best outfit in her backpack. She seemed to have fallen terribly out of practice with her grooming and makeup skills too after weeks of constantly trying to downplay her femininity to keep herself safe. A lock of hair fell down and covered part of her face. She left it there.

He shrugged with a smile. "Not much to be proud of yet, but give me a couple of years and I'll flash some gold on these shoulders." He nodded at the green epaulets which were currently blank.

Olivia frowned, her smile reduced. "What do you mean, a couple of years?" In her mind she would only have to live without him by her side every day for the next year.

Chaim looked at her questioningly. "You do know I have to be in the force for nearly three years, right?"

Her heart sank. *Three years?* Military service was one year or less in Denmark. Why had she not known this? Had she known and blissfully forgotten in all the excitement of travelling? She could not even begin to process what this meant; for her and for them. How were they going to maintain a relationship with him in service in whatever random, dangerous place for so long?

"But how… What am I supposed to do in the meantime? Will you be able to come and visit me in Denmark?" How could they not have had this conversation before? She could not believe it. This was supposed to have been a happy, romantic date, and now they were both struggling to get their heads around the premise of their relationship's survival.

"I thought you were going to stay here?"

"And just wait for you while I clean toilets in the kibbutz?"

Olivia's ears were ringing. They stared at each other. How could they have been so naïve? They had been so consumed by their overwhelming love and desire for each other; living on Planet Love, suspended in time and place, where geography was not an issue and the full realities insignificant. That strange sensation of stupidity was creeping up on her again. She wanted to slap herself and shake that supposedly bright, promising future lawyer back into her mind and body. Her sense of reality and judgment skills had gone completely haywire. She rubbed her temples and closed her eyes.

Chaim sighed and looked down at his hands. "Of course not. I had thought maybe you could study here – in Jerusalem or Tel Aviv..."

"But I don't know anyone here. What about my friends and family back home?" She thought of her grandmother who was unwell, and her parents were not getting any younger either. Despite all their differences, they were the only safe haven she had known. Till now. She desperately wanted to be with Chaim, but was she willing to give up her entire life for him? Hannah and Lola would be going home soon, as would the other volunteers, just as she had planned to do. Naomi and her few other local friends would be in the army, just like Chaim. Was she to start all over at a strange university where she did not know what subjects to study or even the language? Was she ultimately going to live in Israel for the rest of her life? What were Chaim's plans for the future? Her mind was racing her heart in a battle none of them seemed able to win. He looked disappointed and hurt.

"But... I thought you loved me. Like I love you?" His brows were furrowed, his head shaking slowly. His sudden insecurity was out of character, but he did not seem to care. They were both forced into confrontation by the limited time available to them and the emotional intensity of their reunion.

"Of course I love you! I have never loved anyone like I love you!" She struggled to control her voice. "But I'm signed up at the university in Copenhagen. I need to go back to study and work – like proper work."

"So me being in the military is not proper work?"

"That is not what I'm saying at all…" She leaned forward to touch him, but he pushed his chair back. He looked around the café at the crowd. His eyes were wary.

"I think we should leave."

A lump was growing in her throat.

"No! Why? Just wait, and let's…"

"Let's what? I don't want to be having an argument with you – and especially not among all these strangers." He got up and found his wallet in his pocket, frowning as he glanced at the other café guests again.

Her heart was pounding. This was not what she had envisaged at all. Their food had just arrived, but she had lost all appetite.

"Are you angry with me?" Her bottom lip quivered.

"No, I'm not angry…" Chaim grinded his teeth, his whole body tense, then took a deep breath and shook his head. "Just really frustrated. I want us to be together, and I can't work out a solution here right now. I don't have much time before I have to be back at the base. Let's just get out of here." She was relieved when he grabbed her hand. She had plans and ambitions which she did not want to lose, but she did not want to lose him either. She wiped a tear off her face and squeezed his hand.

They had only walked a few hundred metres down the street when it happened. An alien, ear-piercing sound. An explosion so loud right behind them. The force hurled them to the ground. Chaim threw his body over hers. Pieces of debris were falling around them; dust and smoke; the heat from the flames. People were screaming and shouting, running and falling. Olivia could not breathe. Her heart was pounding in her throat and the weight of Chaim on top of her was pushing the air out of her lungs. Her mind was racing. Her gut was churning. She had to get up and run, but she did not know if it was safe.

"Are you okay? Are you okay?" Chaim's voice sounded in her ear.

She tried to reply, but her voice broke. She could not form a single word, just started crying and shaking. Her mouth felt like it was stuffed with dirt. Her vision was blurred.

Chaim got to his knees and helped her up to sitting, all the while rapidly scouring their immediate surroundings. A huge cloud of dark smoke rose up behind him from the entire area surrounding the café.

"Are we safe?" She heard her own voice, muffled as if her head was deep under water. She could hear sirens in the distance coming closer.

"Not sure. We have to get away from here. Are you okay to walk?"

Her brain scanned her body and tried to put it in motion. She stumbled to her feet with Chaim's support. Her body was sore, but she was okay. Physically at least. She noticed blood stains on his clothes.

"Are you hurt?" She stared into his eyes. The panic was taking hold of her.

"No, I'm fine. Just a few scratches."

There were bodies in the street; torn off limbs; stray shoes and bags; broken glass; metal pieces; and so much blood – everywhere and in all shades. Fresh blood. Dusty blood. Dirty blood. She had never seen anything like it. She felt faint. Anywhere she turned her head there was disaster. The smell of burning – buildings, people, random objects – stung her nostrils at each breath she took. She wanted to close her eyes and wake up from this surreal nightmare. The terrifying scenario her parents had dreaded and the media painted had come true. But she was alive; Chaim was alive. That was all that mattered.

They made their way to one of the ambulances at the edge of the disaster zone and both got checked over by the paramedics. The police took their statements, shaky and incoherent; Olivia even struggling to find the words in English; the event too close to make sense of it all. It was a suicide bomber, they were told. The fire brigade and bomb experts had already located the potential perpetrator – or what was left of this person – in the centre of the scene. The metal nails, screws and nuts in a lot of the victims supported their preliminary conclusion. Olivia tried to go over the sequence of events and to recall the faces of the people who had surrounded them in the café, but she failed. Her head hurt, her mouth was dry, her clothes stuck to her body. She needed to get back to the hostel to get changed before her return journey to the kibbutz with the girls. Chaim had to report back to his base. It was the worst goodbye ever.

The long bus ride back was torture. Her chest was hollow. Her face was pale. Her body and mind were in pain. Olivia's physical injuries were minor considering the grand scheme of things. She was paranoid about the other people on the bus. What if one of them carried a bomb too? Would she ever feel safe again in public spaces? Her thoughts ran in a continuous loop, processing and digesting the terrible things she had seen. *You never think something like this can happen to you.* The relentless nausea returned. Who would do such a sick thing? What kind of person was at the centre of so much devastation? What compelled a human being to hurt others in this way? She knew the reasons why, of course, but she still struggled to fathom the realities. She had experienced the dirty face of the Middle East crisis first hand and its consequences on her own body.

Hannah and Lola were shocked when they heard of the disaster and tried to support her with welcome care and attention, but they would never be able to understand how she felt. Her thoughts did not just focus on what had happened, but also on what could have happened. What if they had not got into that argument and left at that exact moment? What if they had stayed to eat their meal? Would they still be alive? Was it pure coincidence or fate? Or even some sort of divine intervention? Who rolled the dice? Who pulled the strings? Were they all just puppets in some intricate, insane play? She thought of Kieslowski and how obsessed she had been with his musings on destiny and chance after watching his *Three Colours* trilogy; about lives affected by forces beyond rationalisation; domino effects of events out of their control. She could not believe how lucky they had been. She recalled Chaim's sudden guarded behaviour at the café. Had he sensed something was not right? She needed Chaim by her side to process this, but he was the one person she could not contact. Her weakness and helplessness stunned her. She was a winner, a survivor, a fighter. Or was that only the case in her known environment back home? Here and now she longed for Chaim's powerful arms around her, comforting and caressing her, keeping her safe. She remembered how he had instinctively protected her using his own body as a shield against the terror around them. He had been willing to die for her. She knew she could not live without him. She would not live without him. But how were they going to have a future together? Their life-saving argument had been their first about this challenge. She rested her weary head against the window pane and watched the arid landscape rush by as darkness fell around her.

She woke up in a sweat, panting in the dark. Her pulse was deafening in her ears.

"Are you okay?" She heard Lola's voice in a whisper. "It was just a bad dream." Her delicate hand patted her arm.

A dream? It had felt so real; as if she was right back in that horrible scene. The dust, the smoke, the blood. But Chaim had been lifeless when she rolled out from under him. She was shaking. Her cheeks were wet from tears. She had to get up and push these terrible images out of her head, running on repeat like a bad horror movie. She slipped into the kitchen for a glass of water. It was a cool, quiet night. No cicadas in the trees anymore. Just the moonlight streaming through the tiny window. She knew this awful experience would never leave her, no matter how hard she tried to block it all out. How was she to deal with it? No one she knew around her understood. But she had to speak to someone. Who could she confide in? On whose shoulder could she lean and cry? No one could give her comfort, but Chaim; her love who was far away now and confined by the barriers of the army.

She still had not told her parents of the horrific event. She was worried they would freak out and demand her immediate return. She did not want to worry her grandmother either – especially not in her current fragile state. Her instinct was to go home to feel safe again. But she could not leave Chaim.

"You have to go back at some point," Hannah stated matter-of-factly.

The girls were packing all their belongings, preparing for their return to Denmark. Except Olivia. She had not changed her return flight yet, but she had asked to remain on the payroll of the kibbutz for another couple of weeks. She desperately longed to see her family, but how and when would she come back here if she left?

Olivia eventually confided in Naomi. She had grown up in the fear and craziness of this alternate reality. She could relate. She had lost family members. She had run for her life to seek shelter in a bunker. Somehow their chat did not make Olivia's heart feel less heavy. They talked about Naomi going into the army soon too.

"Are you scared?" Olivia's voice was soft.

Naomi hesitated before she answered.

"Of course. But I have no choice, so…" She shrugged then gazed out the window. "My sister came back. And I will come back too." She turned and looked at Olivia, awaiting her response, biting her lip. Naomi's English had improved throughout their friendship, just like Olivia's Hebrew had. They had shared so many laughs in the tongue-twisting process. Olivia placed her arm around her friend's shoulder and gave her a squeeze.

"Yes, of course you will." She smiled and wondered if Naomi had plans for the future too; or if she was just living in the now till her army duties were safely behind her. Would Olivia dare to dream about the future if she were in the same situation? She had been too scared of rocking the boat of their budding relationship to press Chaim for answers. Yet look where that had got them now. The girls returned to their work, washing the floors in silence.

The phone call that evening was the decisive factor.

"Your grandmother... The cancer... She has passed away." Her father's voice broke. Olivia stopped breathing. The hall was spinning. No one to catch her. Coldness enveloped her. Nausea emanated from her core. She squatted down, trying to get some blood to her head. She tried to breathe calmly. The receiver cord was not long enough for her to sit on the floor.

"Hello? Liv, are you there?"

"Yes..." She broke into a sob; an uncontrollable, helpless sob. She thought of her last hug from her grandmother at the airport. It had been longer and tighter than any other hug. Her kind, old eyes had then held her gaze, expressing such love, almost willing her internal strength and encouragement on to her. At the time, Olivia had put it down to her wanting to ensure she sent her only grandchild off properly on her impending adventures so far away in foreign lands. Had her grandmother subconsciously known that she would never see her again? Had Olivia known? She did not know what to say. She felt frozen in time.

Olivia found herself sleeping at Tel Aviv airport three days later. Her flight back to Denmark was at 7am, and there was no public transport before 5am. She got a lift with Naomi from the kibbutz late in the evening to spend as little time there as possible. She struggled to keep her calm through the tedious, comprehensive security questions by the EL-AL ground staff. Eventually she was cleared of any suspicions of potential threats. Yet it was too early to check in her luggage so she ended up sleeping on her backpack in the departure hall. It was the ultimate low point of her travels. She was exhausted, upset and all on her own. She had left the other volunteers and the kibbutz with an empty feeling in her gut. She thought of Charlie's leaving party so many months ago. It had been simple, but sweet. It would have been nice to have had some kind of closure on this chapter of her life together with her fellow travel companions. Most of them had been preparing for their imminent departures, but Olivia's had suddenly been accelerated after wavering for weeks. She knew it was unlikely that she would ever see Hannah and Lola again – despite their intense bonding experiences and promises of future photo night reunions – let alone the rest of the volunteers who would be scattered around Britain. But she had to be reunited with Chaim. She had not even got to say a proper goodbye to him. The last time they had been together they had been walking victims, hurt and disoriented. She was angry that her parents had kept from her how bad her grandmother's condition had got. She was angry with herself for leaving home when she knew she was ill. Her grandmother had assured her she would be fine, and Olivia had believed her, her mind distorted by her quest for adventure. She felt like a stupid, trusting little girl. She should have realised the severity of her illness. She should have been there for her. She should have said goodbye. She should have told her about Chaim. Never again would she hear her caring voice. Never again would she feel her warm hugs. She could not believe it. She refused to believe it. She clenched her fists till her nails cut deep inside her flesh. The physical pain was inferior. It could not beat the hurting of her soul. She did not feel safe in the wide, public space of the airport, but she was shattered from all her recent trauma. Tears rolled down her cheeks till she dozed off into a light, interrupted sleep.

She regretted the moment she touched down at Copenhagen Airport. She could feel it in her bones; suffocating; claustrophobic. She was not just saddened by the immense grief of losing her beloved grandmother and her longing for Chaim. She did not belong here anymore. She was caught between places, cultures and people. She belonged nowhere. She was no longer the same person who had left Denmark four months ago. She was a square peg in a round hole.

9

It was a crispy cold December morning. The sunshine was glorious, but gave no warmth. The closest family were gathered around her grandmother's coffin to say goodbye in private, before she was carried into church and the rest of the funeral party were to arrive. They stood in complete silence. The air in the antechamber of the small church was thick with thoughts and feelings. Each individual enclosed in their own goodbye. It was surreal. It was not her grandmother lying in that wooden box. It was not the warm, cheerful and caring woman Olivia had known all her life; who had made her laugh, kissed her wounds and comforted her when her mother had smacked her or told her off.

As the ceremony progressed, she could not breathe from crying so much. For a moment, she felt embarrassed at exposing herself, sobbing like a child in front of all these people, her sparse makeup running down her face. But she was unable to control herself. The complete release was cathartic.

The mourners moved on to a nearby hotel for the mandatory *smørrebrød*, followed by coffee and cake. For once Olivia wished she smoked; a social habit she could have used to be anti-social; to leave and be on her own for a bit instead of being trapped in a room of strangers chatting, laughing and singing even. It was all very much in her grandmother's spirit, but it was smothering and overwhelming; absurd in a way she had never experienced before. She wanted to be at home, tucked under her duvet, sobbing until the pain disappeared; till this sudden void inside her was filled with comfort and peace. Except none of this would happen. She would dutifully sit in this extravagant room, small-talking, eating, drinking, breathing. The void would never be filled. The longing and absence would exist forever.

The colourless walls of the function room confined her. How could beige ever be enough when the walls of her mind were now teeming with colours? The rainbow of all the impressions and experiences she had collected so eagerly in such a short space of time.

She was surprised at how she struggled to fit in and adapt to returning to her home country. She had expected a culture clash when she arrived in foreign lands, but not when she returned. Everybody asked politely about her travels, but nobody could understand how eventful and life changing her adventures had been. Every day she longed to be in Israel again. The comfort of being back in her known environment was superficial. It was familiar, yet suffocating. She knew what was out there; all the amazing, unique places and people she had discovered and were now a part of her. She found herself analysing every detail of her surroundings as an anthropologist studying a foreign tribe, wondering at its strangeness. Everything looked the same, felt the same, even smelt the same. Nothing had changed while she had been away. Except her. It was not just her physical appearance – "scruffy and plump" in her mother's words. It was her mind that had changed; challenged and expanded; animated and thrilled; and her soul so full of love and pain.

Her eyes caught Daniel's across the room. She had briefly noticed him at the church, but had not had the mental or physical energy to greet him. What was he even doing here? Was he genuinely there to pay his respects or had he just taken the opportunity to come and see her? Her toes curled inside her heeled leather boots. She turned her head and stared out the window.

Nearly a week had passed since her return, before she finally got around to emptying her backpack fully. Each item she dug out carried so many memories she could hardly bear it. She opened her wardrobes and was over-whelmed by their excessiveness. She started pulling out clothes she had not worn for so long, having lived out of her backpack. Luxury brands; designer jeans; party dress-es. They all seemed to belong to a stranger. *When did I even wear this? When will I ever wear it again?* She struggled to recognise herself; who she had been – and even who she was now. Piece by piece, piling up on the floor, faster and faster, the clothes came flying till she burst out cry-ing. Texas was playing on her stereo. She dropped to the floor, hugging her knees, weeping, sobbing to the point where she started hyperventilating. Then suddenly no more sounds could escape her; no more tears could run from her dried-up wells of grief. She felt so alone. Unable to lean on her dear grandmother; her best friends away travelling; her family failing to understand how she could feel so alien in her own home. Her whole being missed Chaim so much it was as if she could not even be in her skin anymore. His deep laugh, his clean scent, his soulful eyes. She ached to go back, to be in his arms again. Loved. Cherished. Complete.

"Your hair is so long and unstructured, *ma chérie*. Split ends too," her mother tut-tutted with a sigh, her fingers letting go of Olivia's lock of hair as if it had burned her. "And are those freckles on your round face?" She narrowed her eyes, inspecting her daughter's exterior.

Olivia pulled away.

"That is what you worry about in a time like this, *Maman*?"

She knew she was not the skinny girl who had left her parents' home four months ago, but round was an over-statement and her looks had been the least of her worries lately.

As a child, Olivia had always enjoyed watching her mother get ready for dinners out, having guests or just go-ing to work in the morning. Isabelle Margaux took pride in her appearance at all times: lipstick and on-trend outfits, matching bag and shoes, jewellery to die for. As a young teenager, Olivia had subconsciously emulated her behav-iour and was often likened to the elegant, elfish Audrey Hepburn. Yet she had got increasingly annoyed with her mother's running commentary on details which Olivia had not got quite right in her opinion – and her food hab-its in particular. Olivia skipped lunch and went for a run that afternoon; to kill time and try to fill the immense void inside her with some kind of purpose.

Hearing Chaim's voice on the phone was a blissful balm to her soul. Accounts of his everyday life put her pain in perspective too. They were an army of teenagers, their life on hold in such formative years, their youth disrupted by learning to kill and avoid being killed. Olivia remembered them on the streets and buses; faceless in their green uniforms, but all individuals with stories, experiences and emotions hidden behind their identical facades.

Sure, Danish soldiers had recently started being deployed to foreign war zones, defending democracy and international peace. She admired their bravery too and recognised the potentially fatal risks these missions involved. Yet they all had the choice to opt out and stay in the safe confines of their peaceful home country. The Israeli youth did not have that luxury.

She knew that Chaim was in principle against Israel's subjugation of the Palestinians. Like most kibbutzniks he was in favour of peace and coexistence, but he could not allow himself to be political. The Israeli army was his job and his life; for now.

"We all want to do the right thing. But the right thing is never clear in war." He fell silent.

Olivia empathised with the Palestinians – families, mothers, fathers, daughters, sons, lovers; all captive in their own land. How would she have felt growing up with fear and violence, suffering and oppression? What kind of values and beliefs would this instil in a person? She also knew it was not a simple equation of good guys versus bad guys, and there were no simple solutions either. The conflict was deep-rooted, complex and more nuanced than any news outlets could portray – in either camp.

"Tomorrow is ABC day. Atomic, biological, chemical. We all have to go through it."

"What do you mean 'go through it'?" Olivia swallowed.

"We are trained to deal with it. Just with tear gas. We have to be exposed to it, to test how we react. So we can handle it in real life."

"But you get to wear gas masks and stuff, right?"

"Some of the time."

His voice was thick. She could only imagine the hardships he was going through. Simulating rope jumps from helicopters, breaking into buildings, opening fire on targets, rappelling from rooftops and hurling grenades into windows. Anything and everything to prepare him to go from routine to emergency state instantly and under the most adverse conditions imaginable. She knew that being in Special Forces meant it was even more difficult for him to share details of his daily doings, but she could tell he did his best to give her a peek into his perilous world. Again she cursed herself for being so far away from him. Living in the same country would still have meant communicating over the phone during the week; but being 5,000 kilometres apart added a strain and longing so palpable it hurt.

"Do you get any sleep?"

"Some. Got five hours last night."

"Have you made any new friends?" She briefly wondered how much the male and female soldiers interacted. Were there even women in the IDF Special Forces? She pictured herself storming into a dark building to rescue hostages, her face painted green and her hands holding a machine gun in front of her whilst she shouted in Hebrew. She quickly brushed the thought aside. *Get real, Liv!*

Chaim scoffed. "You don't really go into the army to make friends."

She thought of Daniel and his six months of army training and fraternising. He had just come back and was already going to a reunion of some sorts this weekend, she had gathered when he had popped by her parents' house to see her again. When would he leave her alone and get on with his life? She sniffed and shifted her body.

"But sure, there's a couple of cool guys I hang out with… We have a lot of time to kill and crazy shit to go through together, so yeah… We bond. Enough about me. How are you?" Chaim attempted a more upbeat tone of voice.

"I… I miss you. So, so much." She struggled to compose herself. She could hear him smile at the other end.

"Me too. I think of you every waking moment. I have a photo of you in my locker. All the guys are jealous whenever they see it."

His love warmed her broken heart, and she laughed for the first time since she had arrived back.

"I will come back as soon as I can. I promise." She still had another eight months before her studies commenced. She just had to find a job and earn some money quickly.

"I will be right here waiting for you, *ahuvati*."

Christmas Eve was an empty experience without her grandmother. Just her mother and father – and Daniel stopping by again to offer comfort and support. Olivia had opened the door and was hovering on the doorstep, her arms crossed. Daniel glanced up at the mistletoe in the doorway. Olivia followed his look and scoffed. Damn her mother and her stupid decorations! None of it mattered. It was the worst Christmas ever.

"Why are you here? What do you want, Daniel?"

"I just wanted to wish you and your family a merry Christmas. Plus, your mother invited me." He looked down at his shiny leather shoes.

"Who is it, Liv?" Her mother's voice called from the lounge. "Oh, Daniel! What a lovely surprise." She gushed and winked at Daniel as she stepped into the hall.

"Isabelle. Merry Christmas!" Daniel slid past Olivia and kissed her mother on the cheeks as she reciprocated; the very un-Danish greeting everyone around her mother had become accustomed to over the years. Unless she disliked someone – then it was a formal handshake.

"And you brought flowers too. Isn't that sweet, Liv? Come on in, darling." She sent Olivia a knowing, yet reproving look as she sniffed the lavish, red bouquet. Isabelle's heels click-clacked regally on the black and white marble tiles, like a queen gliding across a chessboard.

Olivia gritted her teeth and left them to it. *Maman and her conniving plans!* There was no way to avoid this awkwardness once her mother was determined. A few days after her grandmother's funeral, she had gathered her courage and energy and had excitedly told her parents about Chaim. They had both stared at her in silence then changed the subject to their impending holiday celebrations. Her feelings and their relationship seemed to be unreal to them – like a girlish fantasy – even when Chaim called their house.

She went back into the lounge and snuggled up to her father on the vast sofa. She stared into the flames of the open fireplace, the small talk of her mother and Daniel a buzzing background noise which she could not turn off.

"So, have you found a job?"

Olivia clenched her jaw and glanced at Daniel. "No. Still looking." She could feel her mother's stern eyes on her. She sighed. "Have you?"

"Yes, actually. I'll be starting at my dad's company in the new year."

Of course you will. Olivia only just managed to stop herself from rolling her eyes.

Daniel shifted towards her, now hovering on the edge of his seat.

"Just taking notes, photocopying etcetera, but I'll get to sit in on his meetings and all."

He looked like an excited puppy. Olivia refocused on the fireplace.

"Well, that's marvellous, Daniel." Isabelle clasped her hands.

Olivia pulled her cardigan tighter around her. She noticed her father tapping his fingers on the leather sofa, from little to index finger like he was playing a tune. The rhythm was comforting. The long silence in the lounge was only broken when Daniel got up to leave. Olivia and her father both gave him a nod as her mother led him out into the hall.

He had barely said his goodbye before her mother was at her.

"What is wrong with you, child! I did not raise you to be such a rude sourpuss!"

"A rude sourpuss? In case you hadn't noticed, I just lost one of the most important people in my life, so excuse me for not being the perfect hostess whilst I'm grieving!"

"We are all grieving, *ma chérie.*"

"Really? You don't exactly look grief stricken to me, *Maman* – more like a merry matchmaker who should mind her own business."

"I will not take that tone from you – grieving or not!" She looked at Olivia's father, but he did not meet her eyes. He had been a shadow of himself since his mother died, struggling to keep up with his wife's determined efforts to celebrate Christmas as usual. He emptied his cognac glass and slowly got up from the sofa with a deep sigh.

"I'm going to bed." He kissed Olivia on her forehead. "Thank you for my present, Liv. Goodnight, my dear." He pecked her mother on the cheek and left the room.

"Well, then I guess Christmas Eve is over. Goodnight, *Maman*." Olivia had to force herself to kiss her mother, but she refused to let her have another reason to scold her. She was so fed up with her rules, schemes, shallow pretences and keeping up appearances. She was hurting inside on so many levels and wanted to be left alone to wallow in her pain.

New Year's Eve was another anti-climax. Another end to a year. Another fresh start. Although, to Olivia her new year had already begun in the Middle Eastern autumn; not now in the depths of the Scandinavian winter. It had started to snow, but it was not cold enough for it to remain. Soon the ground would be covered in grey slush as the delicate white flakes disintegrated and became steeped in grime.

Her parents hosted a small dinner party for their closest friends. Olivia stayed home and small-talked her way through the five-course meal before retreating to her room. With her own friends being away, she did not have any alternatives. She did not want them either.

She looked through the photos she had had developed from the countless rolls of film she had brought back. Landscapes and landmarks, people and parties – all so distant already. The glossy images did not do her memories and experiences justice; nothing but a modest enabler when attempting to share them with her family. But they would never understand.

She thought of Hannah and Lola and their plans of a photo night reunion once they were back in Denmark. It was never going to happen. They were just too different; their friendship forged by coincidence and as temporary as their travels. Yet their experiences together would stay with her forever; highs and lows, fun times and darkest moments; the memories ineradicable and crucial to her development as a human being. The paradox was peculiar. She did not know whether to be glad or sad that she did not miss her travel companions. Olivia pinched her bottom lip as she stared at the photo of the three of them on top of Mount Sinai. She flicked on, but paused when a broadly smiling Chaim radiated from the top of the pile in her hands. She was instantly taken back to the moment. He had been reluctant as always to let her photograph him. She never understood why. The guy was drop dead gorgeous! She had teased and enticed him, gently poking him with her bare toes, sticking her tongue out at him till he finally pounced at her from the other end of his bed and she had snapped him before tumbling back against the pillows, surrendering to his playful bites and glorious kisses.

The bittersweet pain jolted through her at the memory. Her body ached with longing for him. She felt like a balloon bursting with emotions. Unable to contain them, she broke down crying. Her TV screen was teeming with rom-coms and happy endings, couples holding hands, laughing and kissing. She could not even call her beloved boyfriend who was on duty – his first patrol after two months of boot camp and training. Her chest tightened at the thought of him in harm's way. Everything felt wrong. There was no reason for celebrations. Not for her. Not this year.

Misfortune comes in threes they say. The phone call in the middle of the day set her alarm bells ringing. Chaim only called her in the evenings, so she expected it to be for her father who was working from home.

"Liv, dear, it's for you!" Her father's voice travelled up the wide staircase from his office across the hall.

"Got it! Thanks, Dad," she hollered back as she picked up the receiver in her room. "Hello?"

"Olivia? It's Naomi."

"Naomi! So nice to hear from you! How are you?"

"I'm fine." Naomi's voice was shaky and she did not reciprocate Olivia's excitement. There was a long pause. "I… I'm calling with some bad news."

Olivia froze. A seam had come undone on her jumper. A thread was sticking out like a serpent's tongue. She desperately wanted to pull it out, but could not move.

"It's Chaim. He was in an accident."

Olivia's guts churned. She could not muster a single sound. Just waited for more words to come out of the receiver, tumbling down on her like a tower crumbling, brick by brick.

"It was in the West Bank. An exercise or operation... I don't know exactly. I'm so sorry. I got your number from the kibbutz office to let you know."

"Is he alive?" Olivia finally whispered.

"I'm not sure... His parents did not know much."

A wave of emotions knocked her over. Devastation. Panic. The grief of losing her grandmother multiplied. Her insides imploding, creating a whirlpool of desolation. The suicide bomb had been an omen, the first in a row of unfathomable tragedies.

They were not married or engaged. She was merely a fling, a blip in his emotional life – in the world's perspective; in the bureaucracy of emergency contacts and next of kin. But he was her world, and she was his. Closer than family. Yet she did not count.

What if Naomi had not called her? Would she have lived in blissful ignorance till she wondered why he had not called her back? No, there would have been nothing blissful about it. Just an empty hole in her life. She was eternally grateful to her Israeli friend.

She tried to process the facts Naomi told her, but the information was swirling in her head like broken pieces of glass. Chaim's team had been in the field on a counter-terror exercise and been attacked. Naomi had said a car rammed into the group of Israeli soldiers and there had been shooting. Chaim had survived, but there were no details of his condition. She had no idea what state he was in. Naomi had bumped into Chaim's parents as they were running to the parking lot, off on their journey to the hospital in Jerusalem; together in adversity, undoubtedly faced with the worst tragedy of their lives. Was he conscious or in a coma? Had he lost any senses or limbs? Olivia thought of his deep, brown eyes and his capable hands. So many questions and no answers. Just a big black hole of grief and uncertainty.

She knew that Chaim's Special Forces unit was an intense and risky business – even during their initial basic training at the Mitkan Adam army base. She had also gathered that his exceptional skills, determination and physical abilities had moved him up in the line of recruits, advancing him sooner than expected to riskier tasks. *Too soon!* She sobbed, letting out a loud, primal sound like an animal hurt. She had to get to his side. But how? She had spent all her savings on her travels. She had to ask her parents for access to her tied-up funds.

"No. *Absolument pas!*" Her mother's face was as rigid as ever.

"What? Did you not hear me?" Olivia struggled to control her voice, her composure already in pieces on the marble floor.

"Excuse me, young lady! This is the first time you even deign to explain your relationship with this guy properly to us. You just got back from this crazy expedition of yours, and now you expect us to let you go back? What happened to finding a suitable job?"

"I *have* told you about him. So many times. But you would not listen!" Olivia's body was trembling. "I am not asking you to *let* me go. I am an adult who can make my own decisions. And I'm not asking you for money. I'm asking you to let me access *my* money – or at least lend me some till I can repay you."

"Technically, those funds are not your money. Yet," her father pitched in to the heated argument.

She had never seen her parents agree on anything this vehemently. Everything else they could argue about, but the course of her life, the most decisive action she would ever have to take, and they could join forces on obstructing her ability to act?

"Why are you punishing me like this?" Her eyes were swollen, her throat tight, every muscle of her body tense and her head pounding with pain. Any hope of a rational line of argumentation to persuade her parents in her usual manner was lost.

"We are not punishing you. We are protecting you. Saving you from your own stupidity," her mother hissed.

"Stupidity? Since when did love become stupid? You two of all people should know that love transcends borders, languages and cultures!"

Her parents glanced at each other across the glass dining table. Olivia's snot and tears were gathered in pools on the reflective surface.

Her father sighed. "Yes, we know how young love can consume you completely. But we are also old enough to know that making choices based on love has consequences. Lifelong consequences."

"The answer is still no." Her mother's voice was cold as ice.

Olivia pushed her chair back, ran out and slammed the door behind her. The noise echoed through the hall as she leaped up the stairs to her room. She had to get out of here and had no time to spare. She collapsed on her bed and gave in to uncontrolled sobbing. Her parents had reduced her to a child again. What could she do? Who could she reach out to? She desperately wanted to call her grandmother, to hear her voice, to be wrapped in her comforting words and guided by her clever answers. Never again. The definitiveness hit her in the gut. More salt in her open wound. She reached out to grab a tissue from her bedside table. Her eye caught something blue glistening in a little black box. It was the sapphire ring her grandmother had left her. Blue as the desert sky. A sign from above. Olivia smiled and let out a sigh of relief. *Thank you, Grandma.*

10

Her mind was set. She forced a smile, yet her hands were shaking as she handed over her grandmother's precious engagement ring.

The jeweller, an elderly man with golden metal glasses resting halfway down the bridge of his nose, was thrilled at the sight of such a unique piece of jewellery. Any suspicions as to the validity of a nineteen-year-old selling a valuable specimen like this were kept at bay. Olivia had chosen one of the few well-established jewellers in central Copenhagen who did not know her family well. She had prepared a plausible explanation. Her parents did not have the time to accompany her, but they had of course signed off on her selling the heirloom to fund her upcoming studies abroad. She had dressed for the part in her nicest coat and shiny boots and held her head high. Despite her thoroughly rehearsed speech, she still struggled to look the eager purchaser in the eye. She could feel the tiny pearls of sweat on her upper lip generated by the myriad of spotlights in the shop – and by her pounding heart. She had gone over her decision a thousand times in her head. Deep down she knew the right thing to do was to keep the ring. She could hardly recognise herself and her reasoning as she stood there on the polished floors, surrounded by the light and graceful string music of Handel's *Air*, but she had no choice – thanks to her parents. Her grandmother would have understood, Olivia reassured herself one more time, clenching the beige cashmere scarf draped around her neck and breathing in her heavy perfume. *Sorry, Grandma.*

She cashed in and bought her flight ticket. She phoned Naomi for more details on Chaim's condition and whereabouts. She said goodbye to her shocked parents and embarked on her journey – to the same destination as only a few months ago, but this time under a very different premise. She had nothing to lose and everything to win. Her thoughts travelled in circles and detours on the flight. What scenario would meet her when she arrived? What would the future bring? Her fingers fiddled in the pockets of her cardigan, then paused when she felt the smooth surface. She pulled out her hand. It was the white pebble. She stroked the black line through its middle. She did not know whether to smile or cry. She put on the headphones of her portable CD player, hoping for some musical distraction and momentary peace of mind. U2's *With or Without You* sounded out in her ears. A stray tear travelled down her cheek. When would the blackness and anguish inside her come to an end?

She watched him sleep. He was breathing heavily. Only the sound of the heart monitor's regular beeps and her own breath broke the calm rhythm. He was alive; and still so handsome despite his vulnerable state.

She was relieved to be by his side again and eternally grateful that he was still more or less in one piece – unlike some of his team mates who had not survived the gory attack by the small group of Palestinian extremists. Yet nothing could prepare her for the shock of seeing her beloved like this. The bloody cuts and bruises on his face; the bandages covering most of his arms and legs; the white electrodes across his broad, dark-haired chest; the stillness of his strong body. Her brave warrior down for the count. Once again she struggled with the concepts of war and terror. Chaim's injuries and the death of his young colleagues were such a terrible, incomprehensible waste. And for what exactly? Why could they not live in peace? This constant chicken game of who blinked first; who got to stay on the course; who would swerve; who would get killed; who would win, who would lose… Why could they not all be winners?

She peeled at her chipped nail polish. In her rush to leave for the airport, she had forgotten to remove it. She was exhausted from the journey. She leaned back trying to get comfortable in the plastic seat next to his bed and closed her eyes for a moment. She did not know for how long she dozed off, but was startled by a light touch tickling her hand. She opened her eyes and looked straight into his. They sparkled. Her heart leaped. Her hands were shaking when she caressed his face, and her tears ran unhindered.

"Oh, my love." She leaned over and kissed him ever so gently.

He gave a small grunt of appreciation.

"I'm so sorry."

He frowned and moved his lips, but only a whisper escaped.

"I'm sorry I left you."

"Hmm." He tried to shake his head, but his face contracted.

"Oh, I'm sorry I'm making you speak. I'll shut up now and just look at your gorgeous face." She stroked his hair. He chuckled then moved his lips.

"Stop. Saying. Sorry. Just… Kiss me, *ahuvati*," he managed to murmur. She let out a light laugh. How she had missed his husky voice, albeit feeble in his current state, and that cheeky mouth of his. She showered him with tender kisses.

There was a knock at the door and the sound of a male clearing his throat. Olivia jumped up. It was Chaim's father. He had been there when she arrived at the hospital in Jerusalem and had briefly filled her in on Chaim's condition before letting her into his room.

"Sorry to interrupt you two lovers, but the doctor will be here any minute now." He spoke fluent American. The doctor did not. Olivia desperately tried to decode the words, body language and facial expressions of the three men. All she caught from the subdued conversation was "legs" and "luck", accompanied by frowns and deep sighs. The doctor nodded and left, leaving a vacuum of silence in the small, private room. Chaim's father gave his son's hand a pat. Olivia looked from one to the other, yearning for them to share whatever news they just got with her.

Chaim's injuries were extensive: apart from the visible cuts and bruises, he had incurred fractures in his arms, ribs and collarbone. However, the most serious damage had been caused to his spine and he had needed immediate surgery when he had been brought in. The good news was that the initial trauma was limited to his lower spine which meant he would eventually be fully mobile in his upper body when all his other injuries had healed.

"He is lucky to be alive." Chaim's father sighed. "But he may not be able to walk again. At least not without considerable efforts."

"I. Will. Walk," Chaim stated with defiance, holding Olivia's gaze, assessing her reaction. Her eyes were stinging as they flickered to Chaim's father's, analysing them for any signs of affirmation – or the opposite. He looked away. She sat down on the edge of Chaim's bed, held both his hands and looked him straight in the eye.

"Yes. You *will* walk again."

They both broke into smiles, and she no longer held back her tears.

Olivia found a room at a boarding house not too far from the hospital. She wanted to be by Chaim's side throughout his recovery, however long it would take. She had spotted a handwritten note – the only one in English – on the noticeboard in the hospital cafeteria advertising a room to let for a "respectable young lady". It was pinned right next to a colourful poster with the words "Choose Hope – and Anything Is Possible". A white dove soared under a simplistic rainbow, an olive branch suspended from its beak. She flashed a tight, cold smile then made a note of the address and telephone number on the ad.

The landlady was a stern woman in her early seventies. She was originally British, but had lived in Israel for over fifty years. She was also a Christian, as she had made clear in Olivia's interview. She lived on the ground level of the humble townhouse and rented out the first and second floor. Olivia had her own bedroom and a bathroom in the hall, but had to share a kitchenette with the other lodger upstairs – a petite French girl called Manon. She did religious studies at the university, but did not want to live in the campus dormitories. Olivia was keen to engage in philosophical discussions on theology and any social interaction she could get during this difficult time, but Manon was not much of a talker. Olivia was still grateful for her company – especially on her daily bus journey to the university hospital on the Mount Scopus campus where Manon's faculty was located too.

After Olivia's first two weeks back on Israeli soil, Chaim was moved from the intensive care unit into a rehabilitation ward. He still needed substantial pain management, not to mention care in most aspects of basic human functioning. He refused to let Olivia help him. He always made sure the nurses had attended to his morning hygiene before she came to visit. He could use his hands and arms with some difficulty. Occasionally, she would be unable to fight her impulse to hold a glass of water for him or to cut out his food, and he would grunt or grit his teeth.

"I can do it myself."

She would recoil, knowing she had wounded his pride, but hurting as she longed to care for him. Those moments created tiny cracks in their relationship, but every time they would both realise it and be eager to mend them. They braced themselves with patience and persistence. Yet Olivia still cried herself to sleep most nights, alone in her tiny room, desperately seeking release for all the emotions she pent up during the day. She dreamed of walking through soft fields in golden light with Chaim by her side, his strong arms lifting her up and spinning her around in the warm sun; only to wake up in the dark, mentally preparing herself for another day of emotional challenges; physically bracing herself against the cold that now enveloped the city in the Judean Mountains.

Chaim focused on his rehabilitation with the determination of the soldier he still was. Olivia found a part-time job at a café at the university. She was fully aware that her newly gained funds would run out sooner rather than later if she did not find a way of supplementing them. Other than that she did not give much thought to the future, but focused on each new day and what progress it would bring for Chaim. Except when she was at work.

The café was located between the Faculty of Law and the School of Business Administration. Her heart soared whenever she would catch sight of the English title of a law book in the hands of a student. She toyed with the idea of studying here and did the odd research on the local

faculty when she found the time. Yet she was still unde-
cided and preferred to leave it at that for now.

She did not go into the old town or anywhere near the
city centre. She neither had the time, nor the inclination.
Her memories of this beautiful city had been tainted forever by the horrible bombing. She had never thought she
would return here at all. Now she lived only miles from
where she had nearly lost her life. She tried not to think
of the horrible nightmare. She was too busy focusing on
Chaim and his recovery in between her daily routine at
the café. But from time to time the terrible memories
popped their ugly face into her mind, and she would feel
her insides turn and her palms sweat. Her only escape was
keeping herself occupied.

She had spoken to her father on the phone a couple of
times. He was hurt, but she was certain he would forgive
her in time. Her mother was a different story. Despite their
decisive fight and her emotional departure, she longed to
be with her family. Yet she could not imagine being anywhere but by Chaim's side right now.

Every day she walked across the wide, empty lawns between the sand-coloured, modernist buildings of the enormous campus; the cold wind on her face; alone.

He was in a wheelchair when she came to see him one day.
The image hit her in the gut. She was thrilled to see him
sitting up and mobile – but the fact that he was dependent

on a metal object with such profound connotations and consequences made her soul cry.

He met her with a huge smile. Yet she could detect the apprehension in his eyes.

"What do you think of my new wheels?"

She became conscious that she had stopped in her tracks outside the door to his room and hurried in to greet him with a kiss.

"Wow, look at you all cruising!" she mustered.

He grabbed her hand and held her gaze. "Liv, you don't have to pretend."

She cast her eyes to the floor. Was that grey or blue? She hated the indefinable colour of the sterile linoleum of the hospital floors and its lingering smell of disinfectants.

"I know it's a lot to take in."

She inhaled deeply and tried to put on a happy face.

"But remember, it's only temporary. I will be out of here in no time and walking you down the aisle."

Her head jerked to catch his eyes.

"What did you say?"

He laughed, his husky, sexy laugh. "I may not be able to get down on one knee just yet, but believe you me. The entire universe conspired to let me find you and to keep us together, and I will not let you go. You are mine. And I am yours. Now and forever. Wheelchair or not."

His love was unconditional. Always had been. Always would be. He had not once brought up the issue of money. He did not care if she was rich or poor; if she was working in a café or at a law firm. He never assumed anything. He just loved *her*. And she did the same. She loved *him*. His love made her look beyond all the externalities too and be that person he saw in her. Her love for him made him stronger. They would overcome all their challenges. Together.

She fell to her knees and cried, her head on his lap, his fingers running through her long, flowing hair. She had no words. Just so much love.

"Are those happy tears or...?"

She laughed and wept simultaneously.

"Yes," she nodded. "Very happy tears." She wiped her eyes and nose on her sleeve – an image of her mother reprimanding her flashing through her mind for a split second – then cradled his face in her hands. "Chaim Rosen, I love you with all my heart, and I would be honoured to be yours forever." They sealed their pact with the longest kiss.

Spring was in the air the first time she took him outside. The sun was gaining strength day by day; the leaves appearing on the trees in the small courtyard; the birds chirping, busying themselves around the wooden benches. They both sat with closed eyes in silence, soaking up the mild rays, breathing in the fresh air – a welcome respite from the eternal, suffocating smell of hospital they were living in; Chaim in particular.

"I had forgotten how it felt."

"Hmm?" Olivia loosened her scarf.

"The wind on my face."

She held his hand and gave it a squeeze. He had not been outdoors since that devastating day. Olivia had taken him for a few walks in the hallways of the hospital, both of them getting acquainted with the ins and outs of manoeuvring his wheelchair about.

He worked with the physiotherapist every day, strengthening his muscles gradually, but slowly. Everyone was elated that his lower body had regained some mobility, but Olivia could tell that Chaim was frustrated by the lack of more significant progress; his large, athletic body roaring to burst out of its current state of confinement.

"They have suggested an operation."

"What?" She opened her eyes wide. His were still closed.

"On my spine."

She swallowed. "Why? To do what?"

"To try to relieve the pressure on the nerves that are still causing pain, making it difficult for me to control my legs. To actually start walking."

Olivia tried to breathe calmly. "But what are the risks?"

Chaim opened his eyes and turned his head to catch hers.

"You know what the risks are, Liv."

Her heart was pounding. Why did they never share this vital information when she was there with him? Why did she have to keep finding these things out second hand, in bits and pieces, trying to make sense of it all on her own?

"No, Chaim, I do not. I need to know exactly what your options are, and the risk assessments and probability rates and, and… I have a right to know!"

He interlaced his fingers with hers and smiled.

"I know. I will make sure they explain it all to you. In English." He sighed. "But the choice is still mine to make."

The lump in her throat made it impossible for her to respond. She closed her eyes again and leaned back against the hard bench for a moment.

"Liv?"

She took a deep breath before she opened her eyes and straightened up. She adjusted the woollen blanket over his legs.

"Let's get you inside before you get too cold."

Chaim grabbed her hands, leaned his forehead against hers and kissed her.

"I love you, you know."

She ran her fingers through his dark, thick hair. It had grown longer and become curly over the last few months, his crew cut a thing of the past.

"Well, that's lucky. Because I love you too."

"Decompression surgery is used to treat compressed nerves in the lower spine. The surgery aims to improve symptoms such as persistent pain and numbness in the legs caused by pressure on the nerves of the spine. Decompression surgery is often used to treat spinal injuries, such as a fracture or the swelling of tissue."

Olivia read through the papers. She was conscious of the doctor breathing heavily in his chair.

"Any questions?" He folded his hands on his desk. His Israeli bluntness was particularly offensive – even for a direct Dane like her.

"What are his probabilities? Risks versus improvement rates. I need some numbers."

"Well, we cannot say anything for sure, of course. Chaim's initial operation and recovery went well, and we managed to stabilise the spine. We are still in the early stages of his rehabilitation. Delayed decompression surgery can be successful, but like all types of surgery it carries risks of complications."

"What kind of complications?"

"Postsurgical infection and deep vein thrombosis – which can happen after any surgery."

Olivia nodded. The doctor paused before continuing.

"Then there's the risk of damage to the spinal nerves or cord which can result in his symptoms continuing, numbness in his legs or in rare cases some degree of paresis – partial paralysis."

"Paralysis? You mean he would get worse than he is now?"

The doctor cleared his throat. "There is always a risk. Less than one in every 300 operations." He paused again looking down at his twirling thumbs. "And then there is the risk of dying during or after the procedure. But Chaim is young. Very fit and healthy otherwise. So the likelihood is minimal."

Olivia stared at him. *Minimal.* The word bounced off the walls of her brain. What did that even mean? Nothing about Chaim, their experiences together and their love for each other was or ever had been minimal in any way or form. Now she was to rely on this odd, little word as a guarantee for his life. She slumped in the chair, rubbing her face with both hands and exhaled sharply. A metal taste filled her mouth.

She sat in the waiting room with Chaim's parents for nearly eight hours. The longest hours of her life. There were no windows, just white walls around them. She soon lost track of whether it was day or night; they just existed in a vacuum, pending in time.

She thought of her grandmother; how her last moments must have been in the hospital. Had she been in pain? Who had been there with her? Where was she now? Was she watching her from above? Olivia desperately needed her comforting arms around her and her gentle voice to say it was all going to be all right.

She small-talked with Eli and Dana. It was the first time she had the chance to get to know them. Eli had lived in America with his parents from the age of five. He met Dana when he went back to Israel as a young man exploring his mother country. Dana smiled at the memory. It was the first time Olivia ever saw her smile.

The three of them did their best to overcome the awkwardness of the whole situation. They had to move past the initial politeness and etiquette norms. They were all on tenterhooks, their emotions on their sleeves. Any misgivings Chaim's mother might have had about Olivia and her relationship with her son, she seemed to have tucked away – for now at least. There was no room for facades and pretences. They were three human beings suffering and fearing, hoping and praying together. Once more Olivia wondered about the dice of life. Who played them? Were the results down to coincidence or fate? How had she ended up in this waiting room at this exact point in time with exactly these two people and with so much love for another person she could hardly contain it inside her? She thought of her own parents. She daydreamed of the moment they would meet Chaim for the first time. They would be apprehensive, she knew that. But deep inside she also knew – hoped – that they would love him too.

Olivia walked up and down the corridor, killing time. She stopped by to the water cooler and picked up a plastic cup.

"It's okay if you go home, you know."

She was startled by the sound of Dana's voice. She turned to face her, her jerky movement making her spill water down herself. She struggled to keep eye contact with Dana as she smoothed her wet trousers.

"We'll understand. All of us."

Olivia's wide eyes blinked. "Excuse me?"

"If he can't walk again. We understand if it's too much for you to handle."

Olivia glared at her, heat washing over her like a wave, her hands started to shake. Olivia had clearly misjudged Dana's subdued friendliness earlier in the day. She had been raised to be polite and respectful, but she struggled to hold back her instinctive response. She opened and closed her mouth. Did Chaim's mother really think she had not reflected on the consequences of Chaim's surgery? The past week all the possible scenarios had been spinning around in her head, making her dazed and nauseous from the range of emotions they induced; fear, sorrow, hope, elation. Yet one thing was certain: She would never leave Chaim again. Olivia took a deep breath.

"Do you also understand then that I love Chaim? Do you understand that our love will overcome anything – and anyone – trying to keep us apart?" She took a wide stance, facing Dana full on now. Dana gave her a forbearing smile which failed to reach her eyes.

"Well, time will tell."

Olivia felt like slapping her in the face. Instead she turned and walked away, refusing to let Dana see her tears welling up. She sat by herself the following hours, curled in a plastic seat, hugging her knees, her red eyes staring into the emptiness.

Finally the surgeon emerged, like white smoke from the papal conclave. All three of them jumped up from their seats and gathered around him. He started off in Hebrew, but soon noticed the distressed look on Olivia's face.

"The operation took longer than expected." The doctor rubbed his eyes. Olivia stopped breathing. "But the outcome was positive."

They all let out audible sighs of relief. Olivia's shoulders dropped, the tension in her body dissipated.

"There were some complications – a dural tear. But we managed to repair it. Now only time will tell if the long term effects materialise as we hope. He is in the recovery room. You can watch him through the window till his condition is more stable."

They hurried to where Chaim was confined. Eli put his arm around Dana's shoulder as they watched their son; immobile again, but still alive.

Olivia had never prayed before today. She did not know to whom or what, but whatever powers surrounded them, beyond their control, she summoned them with all her being to protect Chaim and carry him through this safely.

"Please, please, please, bring him back to me." Her forehead leaned against the cold glass pane. Her tears blurred her vision of her beloved in his hospital bed, diffusing into a white cloud of hope.

Chaim's eyes were bloodshot, his face swollen and a red mark still remained on his forehead from being positioned face down during the long surgery. But his smile was as lovely as ever. Olivia rushed to his side the moment he woke up and they were allowed into his room.

"How are you feeling?"

"Been better." His voice was hoarse.

"Can I kiss you?"

He chuckled softly. "Always, *ahuvati*."

His lips were dry, but welcomed hers like long lost lovers reunited.

"Would you like some water?"

"Mm."

Olivia held the lidded cup and helped him manoeuvre the straw in between his lips.

"Back to square one." He sneered.

"No. Just a minor setback. A bump in the road to full recovery." She pulled her strength together to muster an encouraging smile.

"Hmm." His fingertips caressed her hand, resting on the bed by his side. "You look tired, my love."

"Don't worry about me. I'm okay." She gave her head a little shake and gently squeezed his hand. She could feel Dana's eyes on her.

"You're stronger than you look, Liv."

"Yes, I am. And don't you forget it." She felt like falling apart, right there on the hospital floor, exhausted from the worry and fear, but all his love and faith in her kept her standing, tougher than ever. He was her pillar of strength; and she was his.

"Whatever happens, we will face it together. Now and forever." She bent down and kissed his forehead.

11

April came and nearly went before Chaim left the hospital. They had received his few private belongings from the military barracks, including a note signed by his whole platoon and his lieutenant wishing him well. Except two names were missing: Yaron and Gideon, his team members who did not survive the attack. He grieved the loss of his friends in his own way. Silently and with moments of reflection, during which Olivia knew she could not reach him and had quickly learnt not to even try. Once in a while he would share little anecdotes about them and their time together as a team, undertaking gruelling training or hanging out in their barracks. She would listen intently and join in his subdued laughter.

Chaim walked out of the hospital. No crutches or walking stick – he refused – just her arm hooked in his. The press was there, taking them by surprise. A walking miracle they called him. There were questions and comments, faces and flashes; the whole scene overwhelming after his many months in a hospital room. *Eager to feed the propaganda machine*, Olivia thought to herself, her jaw tense behind her strained smile for the cameras.

They went from one bubble to another, returning to the kibbutz; this time travelling in his father's car with Eli calm and chatty behind the wheel. The future hovered over them like a cloud of rain waiting to burst. There were crucial decisions to be made. Nevertheless, for the moment they wallowed in the relief of being able to take the first steps on their new journey side by side.

It was a strange feeling being back in the kibbutz. Together, after everything. Chaim's room was much the same. No one had needed it while he was away. Most of his personal things were packed up in a few boxes in a corner anyway, just in case.

Chaim parked his walking stick against the wall. *Any chance to avoid it*, Olivia sighed. The black metal cane slid down and made a clanging noise against the tiles. Olivia bent down to pick it up.

"Well, let me know if you need anything." Eli dropped the last of Chaim's bags by the door.

"Will do, *Abba*. Thanks again" They gave each other a bear hug, his father more gentle in his touch than Chaim. Olivia recognised Eli's apprehension.

The minute they were alone, Chaim pulled Olivia in, his hands grabbing her buttocks. They searched each other's eyes. She balanced on the balls of her feet, reaching up to meet him in a passionate kiss.

"Be careful. Your back," she paused.

"My back is fine. It's my other body parts you should worry about." He had a lusty grin on his face which she had not seen for many months. Olivia giggled and gave in to his embraces.

"Mmm. I have been dreaming of this for so long, dying to feel your naked body again."

Olivia panted. "Please don't use that word."

"Naked?" He continued kissing her down her neck.

"No, silly." She closed her eyes, hating to say it herself. "Dying."

"Right. Gotcha." He slipped his hands under her top and caressed her breasts. She moaned and arched her back.

"How about 'fucking' – am I allowed to use that word? Because I really want to be fucking my hot girlfriend right now."

Just like that he sent a jolt of burning desire through her body. She had forgotten how turned on he could make her. In all their worries and woes, sex had been gone from their minds; reduced to a physical and logistical impossibility. They had stolen intimacy whenever and however they could in their challenging situation. The sudden return of pure, naked desire and closeness was welcome. Yet neither of them could ignore the scars across his body. Suddenly self-conscious, Chaim slowed down his movements. He paused before losing his boxers. Olivia mirrored his hesitation. Her caresses were feather light, worried she would hurt him at every motion, watching his reactions like an observing naturalist.

"Lose the kid gloves," he panted in her ear.

"Hmm?"

"I'm not made of glass."

"I know. I'm sorry." She flushed and looked away.

Chaim turned her head with his fingertip on her chin. He looked into her eyes and there it was. The connection they had always had; electric and so profound it made her whole body quiver. Their eyes were locked. They both understood the importance of this moment. Their bodies moved in sync, closer and closer, melting into each other.

It was tender and raw, emotional and lustful; all culminating in a joint release, leaving them both laughing and crying with joy. They lay in each other's arms for hours after. Caressing, talking, kissing and dreaming – of the life that was to come.

Chaim recuperated with the help of a physiotherapist and regular checks at the hospital in Ashqelon. It was specialised in treating wounded soldiers and terror victims thanks to its location close to Gaza. He was ready to return to duty. His long recovery process meant he had been transferred from his unit to a Personnel Recovery Unit. His dedicated officer had been to see him a couple of times. He came to support him, but they knew he was being assessed too. Considering the extent of his wounds and trauma after the accident, his physical and mental progress was excellent.

He seemed like Chaim; albeit with a handful of scars across his face and ditto across his body; the black walking stick still a necessary accessory; a bit more pensive at times, lost in thoughts he would not share with Olivia. But he had been broody and hard to read at times even before it all happened. They had talked about the attack a lot during his time in hospital. He had been supported by a great psychologist who had also had a few sessions with Olivia. She knew she had to watch out for any signs of PTSD. He did not seem anxious, though, neither in a waking nor sleeping state; no nightmares or sleepless nights – that she was aware of at least. On the contrary, he was positive about the future – immediate and long-term. She could tell he was raring to pledge his allegiance to the army again; to be back on the team, belonging, making a difference. But her heart was aching at the thought. They had discussed the possibility of him transitioning to civilian life and start studying something, but he was not ready. Despite the intense and dramatic action of his short-lived career so far, the soldier in him was unfulfilled.

Hence, the disappointment on his face was evident to all the day he received the letter with his new mission.

"They have given me a desk job," he scoffed and threw the piece of paper on the table.

Olivia had done a shift in the kibbutz kitchen. She did not quite gel with the new volunteers; their state of temporariness so different to hers, and her life in the kibbutz so apart from theirs. Yet she welcomed the chance to converse with native English-speakers. She had just showered and got changed; the heavy smell of food now replaced by the sweet scent of shampoo. She tied her damp hair in a ponytail and picked up the letter. She could not decipher the words. *I really have to work on my Hebrew reading skills.*

"What does it say?"

"I am to report to *MAZI* – what we call GOC Army Headquarters. Ground Arm Command."

None of that sounded very administrative to her. He saw her questioning face and sighed. "It's basically the HQ of Paper Pushers." His voice had an edge of irritation. "Personnel deployment, planning, training, communication..."

"Communication? Like gathering intelligence and re-laying orders? Could be interesting."

Chaim rolled his eyes. Olivia was desperately trying to analyse what this new role meant and how to come up with a positive angle. More importantly, her mind was racing to figure out what it entailed for them and their future together.

"Where will you be based?"

"Camp Rabin. In HaKirya, Tel Aviv."

"Well, that's good news, right? You'll be closer to the kibbutz. And it sounds like you'll be working close to the decision-makers too?" *And there's a university,* Olivia thought to herself, *with a Law faculty open to international students...* She had done her research with the help of a study counsellor in between her café shifts back at the university in Jerusalem. She smiled at Chaim.

"I know what you're trying to do, Liv." He ran both hands through his hair. "But this is not the work I was meant to be doing." He clenched his jaw.

"I know, my love." Olivia caressed his arm. He brushed her off and headed for the door.

"I'm sorry, but I need some air."

His rejection stung like a sea of jellyfish, their poison-ous tentacles encompassing her heart. She slumped down on the bed. Where were they headed? As a couple and as individuals? Should she stay or should she go? So many unknowns and so many choices to make; choices that would determine their future; her future. She had thought they were over the worst. Despite their positive mindsets, the uncertainty generated in the aftermath of Chaim's recovery had in fact rendered them both vulnerable and on edge, like tightly-wound springs just waiting to go off at the slightest touch. Fate continued to test them.

Her life had been so simple once; the most intense sources of pressure being to get good grades and survive her exams; her biggest concern being which university and subjects to choose and which fashionable outfit to wear tomorrow. She sneered at the thought of her old self. Now she was... What was she? She felt like a completely different person, but she struggled to put her change into thoughts and words. She rubbed her brow with her fingertips. A button came off her thin cardigan, dropped to the floor and rolled across the tiles till it disappeared under a large chest of drawers.

"Damn it!" Olivia got down on all fours, desperately searching for the tiny, golden object in the darkness of the narrow gap. It was impossible. She could not do it on her own. She slumped against the dark wood of the offending furniture and broke into a heavy sob. She looked out the window and saw the clouds drifting by on the bright spring sky. She was taken back to that evening under the carob tree when their relationship had been untainted by tragedy, bitterness and inconceivable challenges; a time of innocence and hope. Were they truly different people now? Were they ever to find that pure love again?

The sun was setting before Chaim came back to his room. He startled her as he flung open the front door. She wiped her wet, swollen face and got to her feet, searching his face for answers.

"Where have you been?" She cursed herself for sounding so whiney and needy. *Pull yourself together, girl!* She wondered where that fierce, independent woman inside her had gone. She straightened her back as he walked towards her and brushed her loose locks away from her face. The scent of his body – that intoxicating mix of clean soap and warm testosterone – made her knees weak. He cradled the back of her neck and ran his fingers through her hair as he looked deep into her soul. Then he smiled and bent down to kiss her ever so tenderly. Her body relaxed and she put her arms around his broad back.

"Walk with me," he whispered, then led her by the hand into the evening sun.

"I have been thinking. And I had a long talk with my dad. And my mom too, actually."

Olivia's senses were fully alert. She had steered clear of Dana since their return to the kibbutz. This conversation could have so many possible outcomes.

"If I'm just going to sit in an office for the next few years, I might as well quit the army now that I have the opportunity and get on with my life. I wasn't built for shuffling paper from one pile to another or staring at a computer day in and out." His voice was raised and his gestures agitated. Olivia hugged herself in the cool evening air.

"My accident and recovery both happened for a reason. The universe is trying to tell me something. I do have a calling in life, but it's not to fight. It is to cure, to heal and to help."

Olivia stopped in her tracks. Her eyes narrowed as she faced him, apprehensive, fighting her natural instinct to cross her arms, her fingers now fidgeting against her thighs.

"So, what are you saying?"

"I got a second chance. I need to use it wisely." He looked up at the orange sky then caught Olivia's awaiting eyes again.

"I want to study medicine. All my time in the hospital, my operations, my interaction with the doctors and other patients. I believe I can play a role in it all. An important role. Make a difference to others."

Olivia smiled with an open mouth. She was speechless.

"But most importantly, I want to play a role in your life. Every day. I want us to be together. Now and always. The thought of us being apart again eats me up from the inside." Chaim gave her an intense look then inhaled deeply before kneeling down on one leg. Only then did she notice they were under the carob tree. She swallowed. Her heart beat faster.

Out of his pocket he conjured a delicate gold ring with a sparkling white diamond.

"Liv, *ahuvati*. My love, my life. Will you be mine forever?"

Olivia's jaw dropped. All she could do was gape at him, processing all the emotions gathering strength inside her, bouncing and bubbling till she could no longer contain them. She clasped her mouth with both hands and started crying.

"I told you I would get down on one knee." He winked and they both burst out laughing.

He stood up and held her in his solid arms, his forehead resting against hers.

"So, is that a yes, Miss Margaux-Alexander?"

"Yes! Of course, it's a yes! It has always been a yes." Her body was exploding with happiness and she gave little jumps on the spot. Their lips met in a thousand kisses, showering one another with affection, confirming their everlasting love.

She admired the twinkling exquisite piece of jewellery cradled in Chaim's big hand.

"It's from my grandmother. My dad just gave it to me."

Her eyes opened wide, taking it all in as he slid the ring onto her trembling finger. It fit perfectly and Chaim's smile widened.

"It's beautiful!" Olivia beamed. "Thank you." Her voice cracked. She threw her arms around his neck and they held each other close in the euphoric sunset.

The gods – or two old women – had to be smiling down at them from above, turning fate's punchline into a happy ever after.

Planning their future was one thing. Executing the plans was another challenge.

Although Olivia found Judaism beautiful and fascinating, converting was too extreme for her, especially as neither of them were religious beyond their basic cultural affiliation. They were both happy with having a civil ceremony at a city hall. The big question was where to have it. The answer soon became evident: Marriages in Israel could only be performed by the religious authorities, and couples could only be married if they shared the same religion.

Once more, Olivia was frustrated by the extent to which religion could be a source of conflict and an obstacle rather than a driver for love and peace. The good news was that civil and interfaith marriages entered abroad were still recognised by the Israeli state. This left them with only one option: going to Denmark to get married. Deep inside, Olivia was thrilled. She would be married in her home country. Her family would definitely be able to meet and get to know her husband-to-be. And maybe she would still be able to study in Copenhagen. With Chaim being granted a full release from military service to their great relief, they were now free to go anywhere in the world. Yet he was sceptical of going to a country where he did not speak the language and knew little of the culture.

"How do you think I felt when I came here?" Olivia gesticulated at the window of their room, the green lawns of the kibbutz spreading out beyond it.

"It's not the same…"

"How is it not the same?"

"Because…" He shrugged.

"What? We don't have to stay there. We are just going to get married. After that, the world is our oyster."

"So we're not coming back here?"

"I don't know… Maybe. We have to look at our options."

They stared at one another, reflecting for a while, then Chaim sighed.

"I think we should find some neutral ground. To study. And maybe settle down."

"Like where?" Now Olivia was the sceptic one.

"Like… the US. I have cousins there. In Boston." He looked like he was having a lightbulb moment. He grabbed her hands and squeezed them.

"That's what we'll do. We'll go to Boston!" His eyes were glowing.

"Boston?" His enthusiasm was infectious, but her mind was still processing the whole idea. She knew next to nothing about the city – she had never even been to America.

"You want to study law, right? I want to study medicine. What better place than at Harvard?"

Harvard? How on earth were they going to get into Harvard, let alone pay for their studies? Were they not too late in the year for applying? All her classes and books would be in English. And American common law was so different to European civil law… Olivia struggled to match his excited smile as her thoughts swirled around in her head.

"But how are we going to afford it all?"

"Scholarships!" Chaim's eyes widened and sparkled. "Both my cousins are there on scholarships. There are loads of funds we can apply for. They'll know how." Chaim pulled her up from the chair by her hands, gave her a spin and twirled her back into his muscular arms where he planted a big kiss on her hesitant lips. "We'll be fine. We'll go on a great, new adventure together – somewhere safe – as husband and wife!"

They both started laughing, and Olivia conceded – it was an exciting plan, and she was ecstatic to pursue it with Chaim by her side.

The university application process was overwhelming. Where were they to start? Chaim phoned his cousin, Ohad, for advice. The information he came back with was disheartening. There were no easy tricks or shortcuts, just a lot of hard work, passion and some luck. Olivia and Chaim had to prove their potential based on their modest nineteen years of living life.

"Phew, admission rates below 10%." Olivia shook her head.

"We have to convince them in our applications that we are going to continue to succeed and achieve great things at university – and beyond." Chaim's spirits did not seem dampened. Olivia's head was spinning, trying to grasp all the information and to find a way forward through the forest of facts. On top of it all, they turned out to be too late to meet the application cut-off date in January. It took till June for the college to process the materials, receive further test results and make their final decisions on candidates, but it looked like they had missed the boat for an autumn start this year. She fiddled with her ring. She was still familiarising herself with the feeling and weight of it on her finger.

"You've got excellent grades, right?"

"Sure. I guess," said Olivia with a shrug.

"I've got outstanding records from the army – the short time I was there." His one eyebrow gave a slight lift. "All the interviews and tests screening me for Special Forces… And they can't beat my miraculous recovery for persistence and strong character." He flung his arms out as if he had just presented to her the grand finale.

"Very true." She smiled. She admired his tenacity and enthusiasm. With him she felt she could conquer the world. "I've been thinking, though… Maybe I should speak to my dad?" Olivia glanced down at her hands. She niggled the skin at the edge of her finger nail. She knew her father's name carried significant gravitas in the international academic community, but she had always been adamant to make it on her own, casting off any yoke of expectations or bias.

"Do it! Whatever it takes, Liv. We have to pool our strengths to win this battle." The soldier still lived fervently in his heart.

Harvard was the magic word. She could hear the relief and elation in her father's voice. He was certain even her mother would be able to admit that their plan was admirable, ambitious and worth supporting. Not only did he agree to write a letter to his colleagues at Harvard, putting in a good word for them both and trying to circumvent the application deadline in some miraculous manner by explaining their exceptional circumstances; he also ended their conversation by promising to release her trust fund.

"The money was earmarked for your studies after all."

She could picture him smiling contently in his study, leaning back in his leather chair gazing dreamily at his rows upon rows of leather-bound law books on the walls. Olivia bounced and beamed as she hung up the receiver. A lightness spread in her chest carrying her down the stairs from the dining hall. She could not wait to share the good news with Chaim. She had not told her father about their engagement. This was not the right moment.

Together they wrote Chaim's story in his application letter, demonstrating his focus, determination and resilience, as well as his desire to practice medicine founded on his personal experiences. They included his stellar sports achievements at school too. They captured Olivia's background, ambitions and track record of outstanding academic accomplishments. They discussed every little detail and weighed every word. They mulled and pondered, argued and made up. They pulled in Chaim's parents for second and third opinions – his mother apprehensive and less generous in her words of advice. They went to Tel Aviv to take the required English proficiency tests to include in their applications. They phoned Ohad and Olivia's father again for their feedback and any last tips, before they finally sent off their submissions, sealed with hope and trembling expectations.

With Ohad's help they also searched and applied for relevant scholarships and grants for Chaim. His parents' limited income proved to be an advantage in the process. Both Chaim and Olivia still expected to find part-time work to supplement whatever funding they would succeed in getting. Housing would be another headache they would have to cure once they knew whether they had both been successfully accepted into the Ivy League halls of academia. The logistical obstacle course awaiting them took Olivia's breath away, and she could not even begin to think of the actual particulars. She tried to picture the city by the Atlantic Ocean with its historical landmarks and the tree-lined campus of the college, buzzing with young people striving to achieve. It all seemed like a utopian bubble floating in the desert sky, the burning sun above and the scorching sand below making it near impossible for it to continue its journey, only surviving on their hopes and dreams willing it into existence.

At the same time, they had to sort out all the paperwork to get married at the city hall in Olivia's hometown north of Copenhagen. Getting hold of the right forms at a distance of 5,000 kilometres was difficult enough. Chaim being a foreigner made things even more complicated. The help of her parents would have been convenient. Olivia's main challenge, however, was how to break the news to them. Should she tell them over the phone to give them time to digest before they arrived in Denmark? Or in person, giving them a chance to meet Chaim first? She tossed the pros and cons back and forth in her head for days. Eventually, she decided that she wanted to do it face to face when the time came. Chaim concurred. It also gave him the opportunity to ask her father for her hand in marriage, albeit in retrospect. With Olivia's yes safely secured, it could not go completely wrong.

She had dreamed of this day so many times. Travelling back to Denmark with her beloved by her side; introducing him to her family and friends; her two worlds finally merging into one.

The adrenaline was pumping through her body as they gathered their bags onto the trolley and headed towards the arrivals hall of Copenhagen Airport. Chaim kept fiddling with his watch. She grabbed his hand and gave him a smile.

"You and me, my love. No matter what."

He smiled and lifted her hand to meet his soft lips.

"You and me, *ahuvati*." He winked and they went out into the greeting masses.

Olivia instantly spotted her father waiving a Danish and an Israeli flag behind rows of people. Her heart swelled. Her dear, considerate, loving dad. She could not help herself, but ran towards him with a lump in her throat.

"Liv, my dear!" He gave her a big hug, then composed himself and stuck out his hand.

"You must be Chaim – is that how you pronounce it?" Her father's English was impeccable – and so was his enunciation of Chaim's name. He briefly glanced from one to the other. Olivia gleamed as Chaim grabbed his hand and gave it a hearty shake. His tall, vigorous frame opposite her aging father was uncharacteristically jittery.

"Yes, sir. Indeed it is."

Her father's eyes twinkled. "I'm Arthur. It is a pleasure to finally meet you."

Chaim reciprocated his warm smile and exhaled quietly through parted lips.

Olivia was bubbling and glowing. "Where is *Maman*?" She looked around the crowd, smoothing her hair.

"Oh, she had some work, but she will meet us back home." Olivia's heart sank. How she recognised those words and that look in her father's eyes, despite his excited smile. Nothing had changed here.

The four of them were in the living room. The small talk was running smoothly. Yet both Chaim and Olivia were at the edge of their seats. They caught each other's eyes, and Olivia gave him an encouraging look. Chaim cleared his throat.

"You have a lovely home," he addressed Olivia's mother.

"Thank you." Isabelle smiled politely, eyeing him with calculation.

"There is something I would like to ask you, sir." He glanced at Olivia's father, then down at the Persian rug.

"Oh, you don't have to call me sir. Arthur is perfectly fine."

They all laughed lightly, Chaim slightly more strained. He swallowed.

"Sir – I mean, Arthur. As you may know, Olivia and I have been through a lot together. In a short space of time."

Both her parents were all ears now, their eyebrows raised to the ceiling. Her mother glanced at Olivia. Chaim cleared his throat again. Olivia had never seen him like this. Small pearls of sweat were gathering on his upper lip and forehead.

"We have a very special bond." He looked at Olivia. She beamed and squeezed his hand. "And we would very much like to seal this bond. In marriage. With your blessing, of course."

Olivia could hear her mother struggling to quench a gasp. Her father was surprisingly stoic. "So, may I ask for your daughter's hand in marriage, sir? Arthur?"

There was a moment's silence. Her father remained calm. He looked at his wife then at Olivia, before he answered.

"Well, Chaim. We do not know you very well. Or at all. Yet. But from what I have gathered, you seem like a very decent young man. Brave and resilient. But most importantly, you seem to respect and love our daughter. Thank you for asking me such a crucial question. My answer would have to be…" Her father always took pride in his dramatic pauses, but this time Olivia could have screamed for leaving them hanging longer than necessary.

"Yes. You have our blessing."

"Well, that's lucky." Chaim released a shaky breath. "She's already said yes." He smiled and eased back into his confident self like a majestic tree shaking off a summer shower of rain.

"Has she now?" Olivia's father turned to his daughter, raising his eyebrows. She radiated with delight.

"That explains the sparkler on your finger, my dear." Her mother's eyes glistened, but that was the extent of her approval. Silent acceptance, perhaps. Olivia knew her mother well enough to know that any objections would be communicated swiftly. All she could do was wait and see.

"Well, I believe this calls for some champagne, don't you agree, Isabelle?" Arthur smiled and got up to congratulate the young couple.

Isabelle gave a measured nod and left the room.

"Do you need a hand?" Olivia called after her. No reply. She gave Chaim an apologetic look and followed her mother out into the kitchen.

"So, what do you think?"

"About what?" Her mother glanced at her as she pulled a Veuve Cliquot out of the wine fridge.

"Well, Chaim. Us getting married. Everything! Don't you have anything to say?"

Her mother shrugged with a sigh.

"What can I say, my dear? He is handsome – even with all the scars. Your ring is decent. *Voila!*"

"That's it?"

"Olivia, *ma chérie*. Whatever I say, you will hate me." Her mother made a dramatic, sweeping gesture. "You are young. He is young. You have no degrees. No jobs. No income. You have your whole life ahead of you still. Why rush things like this?"

The anger and resentment fought to conquer her.

"Because I love him, *Maman*! And he loves me. And…"

"Love? Love is deceiving." Isabelle waved her off.

Olivia froze. She stared at her mother, the flesh and blood from which she came. She could hear her own rapid breathing through her flared nostrils. She tried, but failed to regain control of her emotions under her mother's disdainful glare.

"Love conquers all!" Olivia thumped the polished kitchen counter with her palm. The impact sent a jolt through her body. Isabelle flinched and clutched the champagne bottle.

"Yes, we are young. Does that mean our love does not count? Does your age give you monopoly on true love? Who is deceiving whom then?" Olivia's heart was thumping in her throat. "After everything Chaim and I have been through – none of which you can even begin to understand – and with everything we have planned for our future, being married gives us a unity which no one can break. No wars. No bombs. No families. No authorities. None of that will break us apart. Ever again."

Isabelle was taken aback. Olivia had not meant to raise her voice or launch a tirade, but she had had no choice. Somehow that was not what appeared to put her tough mother off kilter. She could see the realisation in her eyes; that her daughter was no longer an innocent child, protected from the evils of the world. She had suffered. She had been exposed. She had seen things her mother could not fathom. Her mother no longer had the upper hand in the balance sheet of life. A moment of silence passed. A nerve twitched on Isabelle's face. Then she placed her manicured hand on Olivia's and held her gaze.

"Then you belong together, and together you shall be."

Olivia's mouth gaped. A grin spread across her lips.

"Now let's crack open this champagne. We can't leave our men waiting." Isabelle tossed her glossy, coiffed hair into place and marched off with the tray, the sound of shaking glasses echoing down the hallway.

12

It was a perfect Danish summer's day. The air was warm. The ivy glistened on the ivory walls of the local city hall. Olivia wore white; a lace top with narrow straps under a tailored satin jacket; a matching knee-length skirt teamed with royal blue heels. Her dark hair was now long enough to braid, and she had gathered her plait in an elegant chignon resting at the back of her neck. She was happy with the final result – despite her mother's objections that she should go to a proper hairdresser. She had borrowed a pair of simple diamond earrings from her mother. They had belonged to Olivia's grandmother. On her finger, Chaim's grandmother's ring sparkled in the sun. She was radiant and ready.

She arrived with her father and gazed up at the main entrance as she stepped out of the shiny, black car. Her heart skipped a beat. Chaim wore a dapper dark blue suit they had bought together in town. Still, this was the first time she saw him wearing it. He looked jaw-droppingly gorgeous waiting for her on the top step of the front stairs. In his hand he held a small bouquet of white roses and sweet lavender. A white rose perched elegantly from the button-hole of his suit jacket. His whole face was split by the biggest smile he had ever displayed.

"Man, you look so beautiful!" He beamed and pulled her in for a loving kiss as she approached him.

Olivia tittered. "You don't look too shabby yourself, Mr Rosen." She still could not believe he was going to be hers forever.

Her father cleared his throat behind them. "Where is Isabelle?"

Olivia looked around her, then at Chaim. "Was she not supposed to drive you here?"

Chaim's smile faded. "She… Something came up at work. An important deal she had to close. I took a taxi."

Olivia felt her heart shrink. *Unbelievable!* Her mother could not even show up on her wedding day? Would she ever get her priorities straight? Her lips quivered.

"Don't worry, she'll be here." Chaim cupped her face in his hands and locked her eyes. They sparkled with love and excitement. He was her rock and always would be. She let out a small breath and her shoulders dropped.

It was a beautiful, intimate affair. The surroundings were formal and minimalistic. Olivia was pleased to see that the mayor's office had arranged flowers on the desk and on a low bookcase along one side of the room. She could smell the lilies as she tried to take a steady breath. She glanced at the white walls with the modernist paintings as they waited.

She wished Chaim's parents had been there. When they had announced their happy news back in the kibbutz, his mother had given them a stiff smile, but his father had exclaimed *"Mazel tov"*, given Chaim a big bear hug and kissed his future daughter-in-law warmly on both her cheeks. Her heart soared at the memory and she could hardly keep it in her ribcage sitting here today on the verge of becoming the wife of her one true love. She had not thought of herself as the marrying kind. Perhaps another silent rebellion against her parents and society, which now turned out completely beyond her expectations. They were not just going to be husband and wife. They were partners in life and would continue to be so. Forever. She glanced at Chaim. He was still smiling, fiddling with the handle of his walking stick leaned against his chair. She turned her head to her father. He gleamed with pride and gave her a wink. His fingers were tapping his lap. Her mother was still nowhere to be seen. The mayor looked at his watch, then at the clerk.

"Are we ready to commence?"

"Just give us one more minute," Olivia's father pleaded calmly. His kind heart always gave his wife the benefit of the doubt. Olivia was not as forgiving.

"Very well." The mayor folded his hands and leaned back in his large leather chair.

Olivia cursed her mother silently. She did not know whether to laugh or cry at the tragicomedy of it all. She could not believe she would do this to her. Despite Olivia's genuine respect for her mother's hard work, her determination and paving the way for women in business, she despised her for it too. The aloofness, the coldness, the missed birthdays, school recitals and gymnastic performances. Olivia could not deny she had inherited her ambition and drive. Yet her mother was not a role model she aspired to be. Her grandmother's caring face appeared before her closed eyes. She had always been there for her. She knew she was there in spirit today too. She suddenly struggled to hold back her tears. Chaim gave her hand a squeeze. She grabbed it, took a deep breath and stood up. He got to his feet beside her and gave her a questioning look.

"We are ready now, Mr Mayor." She held her chin up, sniffed back the treacherous tears and put on her bravest smile.

The mayor looked from one to the other, scrambled to his feet and put his hands together in a satisfied clap.

"Fantastic."

He had kindly agreed to carry out the proceedings in English when they had explained their situation to him. Yet the words coming out of his mouth sounded strange and otherworldly now as Olivia took in the scene. This was it. She met Chaim's eyes. His look said it all. Never had anything felt more right in her life. She inhaled serenely. Her body and mind were at ease now. She surrendered to the bubbles of happiness inside her waiting to burst out.

"You have informed me that you wish to enter into marriage with one another. Thus, I hereby ask you, Chaim Aaron Rosen, do you take Olivia Vita Margaux-Alexander to be your wife?"

"Yes." His voice cracked. She looked up at his face. Her tough soldier was smiling through tears of joy.

"Likewise, I ask you, Olivia Vita Margaux-Alexander, do you take Chaim Aaron Rosen to be your husband?"

"Yes!" Her voice sounded out so loud and clear, it bounced off the walls like a choir of affirmation. They all broke into big smiles.

"As you have now declared to wed each other, I hereby pronounce you husband and wife."

Neither of them could contain their emotions any longer, and they both erupted in tears and laughter as they leant in to seal their new marriage with a tender kiss.

The sudden sound of a lonely applause, accompanied by the click-clacking of heels in high speed travelled from the back of the room. They all turned towards it source.

"*Bravo! Bravo, mes chers!*" Olivia's mother rushed to their sides and showered the newlyweds in kisses.

"So glad you could make it, *Maman*," Olivia smirked. Her mother always knew how to steal the show.

"I would not want to miss my only child getting married."

Well, technically you did, Olivia scoffed on the inside. She refused to let her mother rain on her parade and held on to her smile with all her might.

"Congratulations, my darlings. What a wonderful ceremony!"

Olivia's teeth gritted as she fought the urge to roll her eyes. *You missed the whole thing and left us all hanging, and now you rock up pretending you've been here all along!* Chaim tightened his hold of Olivia's hand. His eyes told her "It's okay." His mouth whispered "Let it go."

"Yes, congratulations, my dear Liv." Her father gave her a loving hug, then shook Chaim's hand with both his. "Well done, son."

Chaim looked like he grew five centimetres taller in that moment. He put his arm around Olivia's waist and held her close. She looked up at him; her eyes, her body, her whole being abounding with so much love.

"I brought the champagne, strawberries and *kransekage.*"

At least you got something right! Olivia suddenly realised she was starving after a hectic morning of preparations, and the traditional Danish marzipan cake decorated with twirls of white icing from their local baker looked delicious in the huge basket hanging from her mother's arm.

"And the rings! *Mon dieu,* I have the rings!" She put the basket down and rummaged through her handbag. In all the formalities of the ceremony, their excitement of the moment, interrupted by Isabelle's dramatic entrance, they had not even given the rings a thought.

Olivia clasped her mouth with one hand and nearly dropped her bouquet from the other. Disbelief, annoyance and hurt all battled inside her. Her mother was the champion of disappointment in her life. She looked at Chaim and he broke into a laugh, shaking his head. "Fate sure has a funny way of giving us her trials and rewards!"

He pulled her in for a comforting kiss and looked deep into her eyes. "But we will come out victorious every time, *ahuvati.* Now let's get those rings on where they belong."

She gave in to the elation as they each placed a golden wedding band on the other's finger; two blissful souls gazing into their equals. Nothing else mattered.

"If you don't mind moving into the adjacent room, please. We have another couple waiting to be wed." The clerk ushered them out after the mayor politely congratulated the happy new family.

Following their brief champagne toasts and light nibbles, they continued the celebrations at a nearby restaurant with a lavish lunch. The starter of fresh shrimps and crayfish on a bed of crisp lettuce was consumed with delight before Olivia's father got up and gave a speech.

"My dear Olivia. We have always had a special bond, you and me. From the day you were born till this wonderful day where you have not only grown into a beautiful young woman, but you are now also a wife. I trust and hope you will carry out this role with as much dedication, love and responsibility as you have carried out your role as our daughter. I know you will continue to be our daughter, but I also know our bond will and already has changed. Another man is on the first place of your podium. And rightly so. This is exactly how I wished for your life to develop, from your first victorious steps." Her father's voice cracked for a split second, and he took the chance to incorporate one of his little pauses.

"Dear Chaim. We do not know you very well, but from the brief, pleasant time we have spent with you so far, I have concluded that you are a bright, strong and honourable young man with the love and commitment worthy of our daughter. We trust you with our most precious treasure. Knowing that although she is fully capable of looking after herself, we take comfort in the fact that you will be there as well to support and care for her through the inevitable ups and downs of your new adventures, most likely far away from here." Her father's hands were trembling now, and Olivia could no longer hold in the myriad of emotions his words had stirred up inside her. She sniffled and dabbed her eyes with a tissue. Father and daughter exchanged an emotional look. Her mother cleared her throat and looked down at her empty plate.

"Right. Before I start blubbering, I would like to raise my glass to this beautiful, young couple, Olivia and Chaim. May you live happily ever after!" Arthur's cheeks were flushed and his eyes glowing.

"*Bien dit, mon cher.* Well said." Isabelle blew kisses to the beaming newlyweds as they all toasted. Olivia got up and hugged her father.

"Thank you, Dad. I love you."

Chaim shook Arthur's hand and patted his shoulder, echoing Olivia's deep-felt thanks.

The wine flowed throughout the main course, as did the talking. They had had limited time with her parents leading up to the wedding, so Olivia was pleased to see both her mother and father now engaging actively in conversation with Chaim. They took a genuine interest in his family, his upbringing and his plans for the future, as well as the unstable situation in his country. She even picked up little nuggets of personal information about her husband which she had not heard before. They had, after all, only known each other for less than a year. *And what a year!* She leant back in her seat, swirling the red wine in her glass, sighing with content, watching Chaim balancing honesty and diplomacy with surprising calm. Her fingers caressed her new ring: shiny, simple and silky smooth. The afternoon sun streamed through the windows of the restaurant, bathing their little wedding party in a warm, golden light.

When the plates were cleared, Chaim clinked his glass gently with a knife and stood up. His tanned face displayed an unusually shy smile.

"First of all, thank you from the bottom of my heart to you, Isabelle and Arthur. It is an honour to become a part of your family. I am very proud and happy to be the one standing by your daughter's side today and forever." He shifted slightly on his feet and let out a small breath before continuing, now holding Olivia's gaze intently.

"My dear, Liv. When we first met, I could only dream of this day. But my dreams became reality, and I feel like the luckiest man on earth. I know that right now in the eyes of the world I may only be a humble farmer's boy. But I will do everything in my power to make you proud and give you the life you deserve." Olivia sensed her parents' approval radiating across the table at the sound of his words, and her smile widened when Chaim glanced at them. *My clever, loving husband.*

"*Ahuvati sheli,* you have been by my side through the absolutely worst time of my life. And I know it was never easy for you. But you persevered and you continued to believe in me, each day giving me the strength to continue to fight for my recovery. I cannot promise you that we will not encounter challenges and difficult times in our life together. But I can promise you that I will always be there for you too." His eyes were wet and Olivia's had long overflown with tears. Chaim cleared his throat and raised his glass.

"A toast to those who could not be with us here today for many valid reasons, but are here in spirit. My mother and father. Your grandmother and mine. And a toast to my strong and beautiful wife. *Ani ohev otach.* I love you with all my heart."

"*Ani ohevet otcha. Jeg elsker dig.*" Her perfect Hebrew declaration of love, followed by her Danish one made him beam with pride. Before she could get up to kiss him, however, he swiftly grabbed an empty glass from the table.

"And now for a small, but important, Jewish tradition, if you don't mind." Chaim wrapped the delicate wine glass in a napkin, placed it on the floor and stomped it loudly into pieces. Olivia's mother jumped at the sound, but her father laughed and clapped his hands. Olivia stared up at her young husband in surprise. Perhaps tradition was more important to him than she had thought. He caught her wide, quizzical eyes.

"Our souls may have been shattered and split, but they have now been reunited in marriage and become as one in joy." He smiled somewhat apologetically at them all, hoping this abstract explanation for his dramatic act held its own.

Olivia stood up, grabbed her husband's hands in hers, sparkled with her entire being and kissed him with longing.

"You are my love. You are my life."

They embraced each other and the world around them disappeared in the warm sunlight.

Despite Olivia and Chaim's objections and attempts to keep their wedding a private affair, Isabelle had insisted that they have a wedding party. Olivia could not quite figure out whether it was out of a genuine desire to celebrate their happiness or her mother's need to keep up appearances which drove her inner wedding planner. Olivia had lost track of the invitations that had gone out in the short week leading up to their civil service ceremony. It was very last minute so despite her mother's extensive guest list, Olivia did not expect a lot of people to attend. How wrong she was. It was not just her parents' acquaintances and business partners who jumped at the chance of an impromptu summer party: A surprising number of Olivia's friends had returned from their travels to enjoy the Danish summer before their studies began. In spite of her irritation with her mother bulldozing her ideas through yet again, Olivia was impressed by the bash she had pulled together in such a short space of time. If anyone had the will, means and contacts, it was Isabelle Margaux.

Chaim and Olivia stood side by side in her bedroom looking out the window, taking in the unbelievable scene unfolding below them in her parents' spacious back garden. People kept arriving, meandering into the marquee, chatting and laughing, mingling about with champagne glasses and canapés served by a horde of waiters.

"I guess this means she approves of our marriage after all," Chaim remarked drily.

Olivia snorted. "That's one way of interpreting it."

"Shall we go down and enjoy the mayhem?"

Olivia smoothed her shift dress. Its cheerful floral print made her smile, and she grabbed his hand. "Sure. Let the madness begin."

Olivia was happy to see so many familiar faces again and even prouder to introduce Chaim to them. Yet the incredulity so poorly hidden on their expressions, the way they spoke to him like he was slow-witted, expecting him to not understand them, and assessed him with ill-conceived stares like an exotic circus animal made her guts cringe. The overbearing looks of her parents' friends and acquaintances were to be expected. She knew this was all a huge surprise to everyone, but she had expected more from her presumably cosmopolitan friends. Perhaps she was reading too much into the extraordinary situation thrust upon them by her mother. She closed her eyes and emptied her champagne glass.

Olivia felt a pair of delicate hands cover her eyes then a female in a shiny pink, tailored dress jumped in front of her. The two girls squealed.

"Surprise!"

"Amalie! I thought you were still in Paris!"

Amalie tossed her long, blonde hair. "I literally just got back this morning! Your mother called my parents who called me, and then I jumped on a plane a week early."

"No way! It's amazing to see you again."

Olivia lowered the pitch of her voice and introduced Amalie to Chaim with a beaming smile.

"A pleasure to meet you," his husky voice enveloped them as he gently shook her hand.

"I've heard so much about you." Amalie raised an eyebrow.

Chaim looked at Olivia. "I think I'll leave you two ladies to catch up for a bit." He smiled at them and headed for the bar. Olivia followed him with appreciative eyes.

"Wow! He's quite a catch." Amalie nudged Olivia playfully with her hip. "So, you think it's going to last?" She narrowed her eyes.

"What? I just married him. Of course I think it's going to last." Olivia looked at her in disbelief.

Amalie shrugged with a smirk.

"What's your problem, Amalie?"

"He's just so… Foreign." Amalie wrinkled her dainty nose. Had her best friend become a xenophobe out of the blue since Olivia last saw her?

"Excuse me?"

"I just wish you had told me."

"Told you what?" Olivia frowned.

"More about him. And the fact that you were getting married. I missed your wedding day for god's sake!"

"We were thousands of miles apart! It all happened so quickly…" Olivia's blood was boiling now. This was not how she had imagined being reunited with her friend.

"Too quickly, maybe?"

Had Amalie been talking to her mother? Olivia felt her chest tighten. Celine Dion belted out from the elaborate music centre behind them. The image of a sinking Titanic flashed through her head.

"You know what, Amalie? I don't have to justify my life choices to you. I thought you were my best friend."

"Exactly! Best friends share everything." Amalie pursed her lips.

"Yeah, well not values and beliefs apparently!" Had they really grown apart in such a short space of time? Olivia suddenly did not recognise her childhood confidante; her partner in crime through fun and failures. She stared at Amalie, taking in her perfect hair and perfect dress. She sensed the vein on her own neck throbbing.

"Ladies, ladies, what's with the raised voices?" Isabelle appeared from behind them, planting champagne glasses in their hands. "*Voila!* Let's toast to friendship!"

Olivia raised her glass but did not clink it with Amalie's. She gave a measured smile then turned on her heel and went searching for Chaim.

They mingled on, arm in arm, small-talking with guests. Olivia gave a running commentary behind their backs, explaining in a close whisper the who's who to Chaim, spicing it up with jokes and anecdotes as their alcohol levels rose in tune with their giggles. She tried to brush off her best friend's bitterness, but it was hard to ignore the tight knot in her stomach. She could feel the tension in her body even with Chaim's gentle strokes of comfort. Was Amalie jealous of her? Was it the fact that Olivia had chosen to take a different path? Or did she genuinely not approve of Chaim? Either way, she could not believe her oldest friend would cast such a shadow over her happiness. She took another sip of her champagne and snuggled even closer to her husband, laughing at their intimate banter.

"I guess congratulations are in order."

Olivia turned at the sound of the familiar voice and stifled her laugh. Daniel had a hostile look on his face despite his attempt at a smile.

"Daniel!"

Chaim froze at the sound of his name.

"You must be Kai."

"Chaim." He put extra emphasis on the throaty Hebrew "ch" sound.

"Whatever."

Chaim's jaw tensed and he placed his hand on the small of Olivia's back.

"He doesn't look very crippled to me."

"I beg your pardon?"

"Did you not rush to his side out of the goodness of your heart, because he was in a coma or something?"

She had never seen Daniel like this, insensitive and obnoxious. She noticed a slight slur to his words, and he shifted on his feet unsteadily. He suddenly seemed so light in colour and build when directly opposed to Chaim. Chaim widened his stance and broadened his shoulders. He looked like a mountain next to Daniel's crumbling quarry.

"I would watch my words if I were you."

"Or what? You'll kill me like a poor Palestinian?" Daniel shot out his chest which somehow made him look like a puffed up pigeon rather than an alpha male.

Olivia's jaw dropped. Chaim's eyes darkened and his fists clenched.

"Daniel, you are way out of line! You…"

Before Olivia could finish her sentence, Chaim took a step forward, prodded Daniel's chest with the handle of his black cane and hissed in his face, "You have no clue, schmuck!"

Olivia's eyes flickered from one man to the other, quickly contemplating how to diffuse the situation before it escalated into something unforgivable. Then thankfully her father intervened out of nowhere.

"I think it's time for you to go now, Daniel." He placed his hand on Daniel's shoulder and gave Chaim a stern smile.

"Charming. Very charming husband you've landed yourself there, Liv. Good luck to you, my dear. A pleasure to see you as always." He nodded with resignation, his upper lip curled in an obscure grin, flashing his teeth like a grimacing chimpanzee. Then he half stumbled as Olivia's father led him firmly through the crowd towards the house.

Olivia noticed another blonde head next to Daniel's as he disappeared. The female turned and caught Olivia's eyes. *Amalie.* A sardonic smirk unfurled on her friend's face as she put her arm around Daniel and left.

Chaim glanced around at the glaring guests and adjusted his blazer. Olivia smoothed her hair and smiled at the closest bystanders.

"I guess not all Danes are friendly and welcoming," he sneered.

"I'm so sorry about that. He's normally a very peaceful guy."

"Huh. Could have fooled me."

She grabbed his hand and kissed him tenderly. The guests' chatter recommenced. The tension slowly ebbed away from both of them, their unity once again restored.

"Screw them all," she whispered in his ear. "Let's go to the bar and get wasted on the free drinks! My mother's picking up the bill, remember?"

Chaim's solemn face slowly cracked with a grin and he followed his half-dancing, cheekily smiling wife through the marquee.

They basked in their glorious joy those following days, just enjoying each other's company as newlyweds; the pressure of organising and the nervous expectations before the ceremony now safely behind them. They talked about their future; and their past. Olivia's parents left them to it, knowing they would be gone soon enough, appreciating their company for as long as they could. Both Isabelle and Arthur seemed to grow a deep fondness for Chaim which surprised and pleased Olivia in equal measures. Any initial reservations were blown away by his eloquence, maturity and balanced views of the world. Olivia carried her pride like a cherished baby, embracing all the positive energy surrounding them.

She could look at him forever, take in his endless beauty, trace every feature of his face and every nook of his body. The big red scars on his torso and limbs, as well as the smaller ones on his face, had all faded to pink.

"Good morning, Mrs Rosen."

His morning eyes and morning voice made her weak with desire. His words made her heart sing. They broke into smiles whenever they called each other Mr and Mrs. She drew figures of eight on his bare skin. His warm, heavy hand rested on her waist. His scent filled her lungs. He met her in a kiss before his tongue traced across her body like a paintbrush on a canvas, mastered by a skilful artist. She melted under his touch and they merged into one.

They visited her grandmother's grave. Olivia had not been there since the funeral. She had a stark flashback to that cold, crisp winter morning she had last stood here, looking down the deep hole as her grandmother's coffin was hoisted into the ground. Olivia shivered. Her absence was as deafening as her presence had been immense. It was the first time she saw the white marble headstone.

Rigmor Vita Alexander
1932-1997
In loving memory of a beautiful soul
Gone too soon

Yes, that was her grandmother's resting place, but she was not there. She could not be. It was impossible for Olivia to fathom that her grandmother's warm, soft body was buried in the dirt below the gravel. She was somewhere else. Somewhere safe and serene. Somewhere her soul could live on in peaceful, idyllic surroundings. Olivia did not believe in heaven or paradise as pictured by religion. But she knew there was a special place where her dear grandmother rested and watched over her. There had to be.

Chaim arched his back and gave a small groan.

"Are you okay?"

"Yes. Just haven't done my exercises for a while." He bent down to reach for his toes and let his arms dangle for a moment.

And you've left your walking stick at home again... Olivia swallowed. Months of worry crept up on her, familiar but upsetting like an unwelcome friend. The black cane was a constant reminder of his limitations; boundaries he was determined to break. Chaim got annoyed whenever she encouraged him to do the exercises prescribed by the physiotherapist he had seen every week after returning to the kibbutz. She had suggested that they both went to the local gym, but time just seemed to be slipping through their fingers these days. She caressed his back as he straightened, gently where she knew his scar was hidden under his shirt.

"Does it hurt?"

"No, not anymore. Just get a bit of tingling sometimes in my legs and feet. The exercises help. And massages." He pulled her close and wiggled his eyebrows. His tall, broad frame encompassed her. She chuckled. He was a hopeless flirt around her. She had never seen him like this around other women, though. He was as loyal and loving as she could ever have hoped a partner to be.

"Well, let's see what I can do to help you with that, Mr Rosen." Her lips met his and their tongues played their passionate game, adventurous, yet at ease with one another. She became aware that they were still in the graveyard and let go of his lips.

"This is entirely inappropriate."

"Hmm?"

"Let's leave." She grinned and pulled him by his hand.

"But I just can't keep myself from touching my wife's hot body. Is that a sin?"

Her heart somersaulted every time he called her his wife and she called him her husband. It still felt like a dream – a beautiful, happy dream.

"I don't believe in sins. But I do believe in right times and places for things."

He let out a small laugh. "Sorry."

"Don't be sorry – I'm not. I will be if you stop wanting me once we get back to my room," she purred.

"Oh, really?"

"Yes. Then I won't vouch for the consequences."

"Is that so…" He grabbed her around her waist, and she shrieked as the touch of his hands tickled her sides unintentionally. "I will never stop wanting you."

She sensed his warm breath on her face and the desire in his eyes matched hers. Their fingers weaved together, and they left the cemetery half running and skipping, the gravel crunching under their young feet, high on love.

"You have to see and hear both sides of the story to fully understand."

Chaim and Arthur were having yet another intellectual discussion at the dining table. Isabelle had come home early and cooked dinner for the first time in years. Olivia had struggled to supress a spontaneous laugh at the sight of her mother leaning over the ceramic stove top, flipping steaks and sautéing vegetables – still in her high heels, of course.

The foursome were digesting their meal and swirling their red wine with Debussy's piano notes playing in the background.

"Israelis and Arabs have very different perceptions of reality. Our values and beliefs evolved from historic developments. Jewish history is full of tragedy. Since the destruction of the Second Temple we've been 'The Hunted Ones'. So our history of weakness and persecution makes it very hard for us to... To turn the other cheek."

Chaim's own cheeks were flushed. Olivia could tell her father enjoyed watching him argue his case as if they were in a courtroom. She could feel Chaim's muscles flexing under his shirt as she caressed his back. She smiled. His enthusiasm was infectious and admirable, yet she had an eerie feeling of déjà vu; a recollection of that soldier in the kibbutz who had been so full of hatred. Her mind jumped straight on to the scene of the suicide bombing. She had tried to picture the face of the perpetrator so many times, tried to understand, but always ended up with blurry images of blood and her gut wrenching. She shook it off with a shudder.

"Do you believe the Balfour Declaration was the right thing to implement then?" Her father was testing him.

Chaim made a slight sweeping gesture. "I'm an Israeli and a Jew. Naturally, I think our country belongs to us. Having the British interfere may not have been ideal in retrospect, but it was the only peaceful option – and internationally recognised too. Except by the Arabs, of course. But the Jewish people – the Zionists – built Israel. Not the British or the international community. And we've been on our own ever since."

"Well, you do have the UN on your side – most of the time. Or you would not have had Resolutions 181 and 242," Arthur countered.

"And the French," Isabelle chimed in.

Chaim snorted. "The UN – are you kidding? No offense, but where were they all in 1948? We lost one percent of our population in the War of Independence! And the UN haven't exactly been biased in favour of Israel for the past two decades."

He noticed the surprise on their faces. He leant back in his chair and sighed.

"Don't get me wrong, I don't think there should be iron walls anywhere in the world today. I wish nothing more than for Arabs, Palestinians and Israelis to live in peace side by side. I don't believe violence or war is the solution to anything – despite my time in the army." His voice lowered as he ran a finger down his aquiline nose. "But the Arabs don't seem to look at it the same way. They will always be hostile towards Israel. At every peace talk we all hope, but…"

Chaim trailed off and threw his open palms out to the side.

"Perhaps the Arabs see you the same way?" Olivia could not help but interject. An overwhelming sense of lost opportunities and meaningless tragedy dominated her thoughts throughout the intense discussion. Chaim looked at her with furrowed brows.

"Well, let's hold on to that hope." Arthur gave a slight nod and raised his glass. "To peace."

"*L'chaim*," Chaim joined in with a subtle smile, putting his arm around Olivia, and the tension evaporated.

The only cloud on their clear blue sky of happiness was the uncertainty about their future. The waiting game was only made bearable by the fact that they were enduring it together. Olivia checked the post first thing every morning, each day trying to appease their disappointment with excursions to sights and museums, introducing Chaim to the culture and history of her home country. They strolled through the beautiful gardens of Tivoli and even ventured to ride the hundred-year-old rollercoaster. They cruised the harbour and canals of Copenhagen, waving to the Little Mermaid and the Queen; Olivia's head resting on Chaim's shoulder, their eyes closed in the summer sun. They took in Kronborg Castle where Shakespeare had conjured up Hamlet and explored the Viking Ship Museum, seeping in a thousand years of battles and boatmanship; their hands entwined, their voices and words dancing and playing, their minds as one, hoping their shared life would last forever.

Eventually, the pieces of the puzzle all fell into place. On the day Olivia received her admission letter at her parents' house, Chaim's father phoned to let them know that his letter had arrived in the kibbutz too – and he had been granted a full scholarship by Harvard. Chaim punched the air laughing, and Olivia squealed with excitement and relief. Her inner explorer had been reignited. Her soul had got an itchy foot, longing to escape again. This time with Chaim by her side. She was bursting with gratefulness.

"Well done, my dear." Olivia's father hugged her as they celebrated the happy news that evening. "Well done, both of you." He went on to shake Chaim's hand across the kitchen counter. "I have a surprise for you." Arthur handed Olivia an envelope. She weighed it in her hands, looking at him with questioning eyes.

"Go on then. Open it," her mother urged.

Chaim peered over her shoulder as she pulled out a handful of flight tickets. Copenhagen to Tel Aviv. Tel Aviv to Boston.

"It's an extra wedding present. You won't be needing the Georg Jensen dishes you mother bought you anytime soon anyhow." Arthur winked. Isabelle gave a mock gasp. Olivia threw her arms around her father, giving him the biggest hug.

"Oh, Dad. Thank you."

"Thank you, Arthur." Chaim gave her father a jovial pat on the back. "And Isabelle." Her mother welcomed Chaim's kisses on her cheeks with open arms. They were all smiles.

The twosome left for Israel a week later. Chaim was happy to see his parents again and keen to pack his things for their new adventure. Olivia was delighted to catch up with Naomi who happened to be home in the kibbutz on leave from the army for the weekend. The couple were congratulated by all on their marriage – even by grumpy Vardit who seemed to have buried any grudges she had once held against Olivia. They were sent off on their travels with well-wishes.

Their final goodbyes were as emotional as the ones they had said in Denmark.

Olivia looked at her feet planted in the Israeli dust, self-conscious as Chaim and his father held each other in the longest hug. She tugged her T-shirt lightly to let some air cool her down in the afternoon heat.

"Thank you." Chaim's mother touched Olivia's arm. The unexpected gesture jolted through her body. "For standing by him." Dana's eyes, soulful and glowing like her son's, locked Olivia's.

Olivia's heart stumbled over itself. Her lips parted. Her eyes softened. A warm breeze rustled the leaves of the treetop above them.

"I always will." She put her hand on Dana's and gave it a squeeze. The two women beamed.

Olivia and Chaim were ready for their new beginning together. Soon their kindred souls would be on neutral ground with opportunities of fulfilling their ambitions: to help people through their studies and future jobs. Olivia was at ease again. She had struggled with her sense of belonging, exacerbated by her confrontation with her past in Denmark. Still, it had been a relief to reconcile with her family and a joy to share her life and childhood home with Chaim. Now her comfort batteries were recharged, and she longed to break free. Away from her parents. Together with her soulmate. This time with the financial security of her trust fund and Chaim's scholarship as a safe foundation for their joint endeavours.

Olivia felt a rush of adrenaline when they boarded the plane to America, her hands trembling slightly as she squeezed her bulging hand luggage into the overhead compartment, her upper lip damp as she sat down in her seat. *This is it.*

Chaim put his strong hand on her thigh and looked into her eyes. He did not have to say a word. Her body and mind instantly became calm. Their fingers entwined, she exhaled. He leant over and she welcomed his kisses. Olivia looked out the small elliptic window at the white clouds soon floating below them. *Choose hope and anything is possible.* She smiled and closed her eyes.

ACKNOWLEDGEMENTS

Twenty years ago, I touched down in Israel's Ben Gurion Airport – and so did Olivia. Like her, I was a young Danish girl looking for an adventure far away from home. Fortunately, I was spared from the dangers our female protagonist encountered, but nonetheless they were always looming over our heads. My life went down a different path, but I too got my happy ending. I hope you have enjoyed reading about the adventurous journey of Olivia and Chaim. Thank you for joining us. Who knows what the future will bring for our young couple...

A huge thank you to my trusted beta readers for your invaluable feedback and encouragement: Bibi, Danielle, Lars, Yatir and Achinoam. Sincere thanks for all the expert advice and insights to Dr Jenny Bedford, Sarah Orr, Dr Martin Fabricius, Dr Jannick Brennum, my excellent editor Freda Warrington and my perfect proofreader Karl Drinkwater.

You all helped my story come alive and balance the fine line between fiction and reality.

A special thank you to the brilliant artist Bruno Cavellec for designing such a unique and soulful book cover – once again you gave my story a face to be proud of. To our book cover models Raluca and Neil: Thank you for your time and patience. We hope we made you proud too.

Last, but certainly not least, thank you from the bottom of my heart to my supportive family and friends who helped me reach for the stars, and above all to my loving husband for always believing in me.

REFERENCES

The author respectfully recognises the copyright of the following works of art which are referenced directly or indirectly in this novel (listed in order of appearance):

"Livin' on a Prayer" – Jon Bon Jovi, Richie Sambora and Desmond Child (1986)

"Mr. Jones" – David Bryson, Adam Duritz, Charlie Gillingham, Matt Malley, Ben Mize and Dan Vickrey (1993)

"Put Your Arms Around Me" – Sharleen Spiteri, Johnny McElhone, David Stewart and Robert Hodgens (1997)

"Barbie Girl" – Søren Rasted, Claus Norreen, René Dif and Lene Nystrøm (1997)

"1984" – George Orwell (1949)

"Animal Farm" – George Orwell (1945)

"Killing in the Name" – Tim Commerford, Zack de la Rocha, Tom Morello and Brad Wilk (1992)

"Firestarter" – Kim Deal, Anne Dudley, Keith Flint, Trevor Horn, Liam Howlett, J.J. Jeczalik, Gary Langan and Paul Morley (1996)

"Indiana Jones and the Last Crusade" – Steven Spielberg and George Lucas (1989)

"Three Colours" trilogy – Krzysztof Kieslowski and Krzysztof Piesiewicz (1993-1994)

"Air" from "Water Music" Suite in F Major – George Frideric Handel (1717)

"With or Without You" – U2 and Bono (1987)

"My Heart Will Go On" – James Horner and Will Jennings; performed by Celine Dion (1997)

"Clair de lune" from "Suite bergamesque" – Claude Debussy (1905)

The author apologises for any errors or omissions and would be grateful to be notified of any corrections that should be incorporated in future editions of this book.

THE COSMOPOLITAN ISLANDER

What if life as you know it was turned upside down? Would you still be the same person?

When Chloe is forced to leave behind her cosmopolitan life in London to move to a small island in the Irish Sea, she is faced with a myriad of challenges:

How will she and her family adapt to island life? Will she find new friends? What about her career? Most importantly, will the love of Chloe and her husband survive their amorous adventures?

Join Chloe on her journey through her past and her present to make sense of her life, herself, her hopes, and dreams amid her personal upheaval.

The Cosmopolitan Islander is a thrilling story of female roles and identity in the 21st century – and about how the journey of life can change your destination in the most unexpected way.

It takes the reader from the Isle of Man and around the world, traversing the timeless themes of love, desire, family, friendship, power, and ambition.

"Absolutely riveting! A richly evocative examination of life, love, loss, and the different ways people react to unusual situations. An entertaining and enlightening ride." - 5 stars, Goodreads Reviews

GOLD WINNER of the Circle of Books Rings of Honor Awards 2016.

Available as e-book and paperback from major online retailers and select bookshops.

Find out more about this exciting novel on:
www.facebook.com/thecosmopolitanislander